YA F
Agui]
auth<
Wonn:

D1234218

)73-

COMING OUT
wonnie

sylvia aguilar-zéleny

E

E P I C
Press

Wonnie
Coming Out: Book #5

Written by Sylvia Aguilar-Zéleny

Copyright © 2016 by Abdo Consulting Group, Inc.

Published by EPIC Press™
PO Box 398166
Minneapolis, MN 55439

Printed in the United States of America.

Cover design by Nicole Ramsay
Images for cover art obtained from Shutterstock.com
Edited by Nancy Cortelyou

LIBRARY OF CONGRESS CATALOGING-IN-PUBLICATION DATA

Aguilar-Zéleny, Sylvia.
Wonnie / Sylvia Aguilar-Zéleny.
p. cm. — (Coming out)
Summary: Wonnie is a brave girl who came out at just thirteen-years old and got
immediate support from her parents and friends. Following a day in the life of
Wonnie, witness her love life at its peak, while dealing with Rebecca, Wonnie's
girlfriend, who wants to settle down and get married.
ISBN 978-1-68076-013-2 (hardcover)
1. Homosexuality—Fiction. 2. Lesbians—Fiction. 3. Lesbian teenagers—Fiction.
4. Coming out (Sexual orientation)—Fiction. 5. Young adult fiction. I. Title.
[Fic]—dc23
2015932735

*To Sofi, who showed me
the rainbows of Philadelphia*

CHAPTER ONE
saturday, three a.m.

"So, I've been thinking, Wonnie. And don't freak out, please don't . . . What if we get married?

I stop battling with the million pillows on her bed. "Married, you and me? You're not fucking serious, are you?" I say. Rebecca and I have been volunteering at the Rainbow Pride march all day and I am so tired, all I want is to go to bed.

"I told you not to freak out. Come sit with me." I sit, and she continues, "I know it sounds like a crazy thing to do. I know you're going to say that we might be too young, but . . . "

I stand up and cross my arms. "It's not that I *think* we might be too young—we *are* too young."

Rebecca pulls my hand and forces me to sit down with her again.

"No, we're not. Women used to get married right after high school," she says, pointing to the picture of her grandparents on her bookcase, right next to her Eve Ensler book collection.

"Yeah, Rebs, to men. Let's just go to bed." I stand up, take off my jeans, and climb into her bed. "I think hearing that old lesbian couple at today's event affected you."

"Well, yeah, maybe. But I have been thinking about it for a while. I know it sounds scary, but we are already a family. You, me, my brother. Besides, imagine what a statement we'd make," Rebecca says as she takes off her clothes and puts on her PJs.

"Statement?"

Rebecca turns on the lamp on her side table and gets into bed with me.

"Yes, Wonnie. It would be a statement validating gay marriage in our state, plus it will also be a way to show our commitment to the movement and, obviously, to each other."

"Wow, how romantic. We would get married for political reasons, then?" I ask her jokingly and regret it immediately.

"Come on, Wonnie. You know I love you." Rebecca kisses me softly and caresses my face.

"I dunno, Rebs. Can we sleep on it? I'm way too tired now. That march sucked the life out of me."

"I guess you're right. I'm tired too. Let's talk about it in the morning, yes?" Rebecca kisses me and then turns off the light.

When we left the march, I just wanted to get back and have sex. But *this* conversation has sorta turned me off. Of course, if she insists, I'll give in. When it comes to sex I have a simple on/off switch.

But Rebecca's switch is off. She makes me turn my back to her so we can cuddle and spoon. We become one body with four legs and four arms. Her face finds a home between my shoulder and my neck. I love sleeping with Rebecca, her body wrapped around mine.

"I love you," she says.

"I love you too." I close my eyes and try to get some sleep, but how can I rest after what Rebecca just asked me? I hope she falls asleep and leaves the topic alone for good—or at least for the night.

Get married? That's crazy.

It's a scary word: *marriage*. I love Rebecca. She and I are perfect together just the way we are. One thought leads to another and my *first* marriage comes to mind.

Back when we were kids, Ericka Gussen was a big deal around the block. One, because she was super pretty. Two, because her mother worked at the airport and promised to take the neighborhood kids to visit the air traffic control tower. And three, because Ericka's father died in some sort of super-dramatic accident.

This was back when I was surrounded by friends whose parents fought a lot, or friends whose parents were divorced and fought even more. Ericka seemed to have been born from a loving marriage that ended in tragedy. I was born into an average family: working Dad, stay-at-home Mom, spoiled daughter.

Ours was a new housing development, and we all moved in almost at the same time. Ericka was the last one to arrive and by then we were all good friends: Mark, Rachel, Jim, and me. We were the kind of friends who would fight to the death one day over a fucking ball, and reconcile the next with a smile and a couple of Gummy Bears. We knew each others' secrets and stuff. We were together all day long. Rachel had Barbies, I had Polly Pockets, but we were always convinced by the boys to play rough, hardcore games like stickball, ultimate ninja fights, and wall ball. We also liked to sit down and take turns telling stories till it was time to go home.

Ericka was the novelty. She was pretty. She was weird. She was like the new toy we all wanted. I remembered that as the movers were carrying stuff out of their truck and into her house, Ericka stayed outside, staring at us for like . . . forever. Smiling.

"Do you wanna play ball?" Mark asked her.

She didn't.

"You sure?" Jim asked.

"We don't bite," I said.

She shook her head no and forced a little smile, which I translated into, "No, thank you, guys, I'm too shy." She stayed there for a while, simply looking at us, and then walked into her house. We went back to our game. If she didn't wanna play, so what? None of us knew about her dad yet so she was just a very pretty girl who did not want to play with us.

Two or three days after she moved, Rachel gave us the news.

"So, you know Ericka, the new girl?" she asked.

"Yeah," we all said.

"What about her?" Jim asked.

"So her dad is dead. *Dead.* He died in that accident, remember?"

"Accident?" Mark asked. I still had the word *dead* in my mind so I missed part of Rachel's story. ". . . And he was in it, and he died. *Died*," Rachel concluded.

"Wait, what?" I asked.

Mark and Jim retold the story. Ericka's dad was one of the passengers in a train wreck we'd heard about the year before. Part of the train landed on his head and he died. No one I knew in my family had ever died. Most of my grandparents and extended family were alive (and those who were dead, I'd never really met), so I couldn't imagine it. Now that I think about it, Ericka became a fixation for me right at that very moment for that very reason.

What none of us knew yet was that after her father's death, Ericka stopped talking for months. She didn't want to be in school, so she was homeschooled by her aunt, and she didn't have friends or play outside. Ever.

My mother is like a one-woman reception committee and soon became Erika's mom's neighborhood guide. If she hadn't, Ericka and I wouldn't have become so close. Ericka would have never come out to play with me, and then with the whole gang, and, of course, she would never, ever, ever have been my husband.

"I invited Ericka over to play with you, Wonnie," Mom said.

"Who?"

And then Ericka with her big black eyes and sad face came into my room.

"Me," she said. Ericka seemed surprised after seeing my mess on the floor. She could not even walk inside my room. Let me add that this was the week after a horrific flu kicked me in the balls, and even though I was better, Mom forced me to stay home. My room was carpeted with shoeboxes and Legos because I had started a new thing: building entire cities with whatever I had on hand. Ericka was there, trying to figure out a way to enter.

"Sweetie, explain to Ericka what all this is," my mom said.

"I'm building a city," I said, all proud.

"A city?" She asked in disbelief. She took like a zillion minutes to observe every object on the floor. Then, she asked, "Is that a restaurant?" She pointed to my McDonald's Happy Meal box.

"Yes. Do you wanna play?" I asked her.

Yes, Ericka wanted to play. She spent all afternoon with me. We didn't talk all that much but it seemed like she had fun. She came the next day, and the next, and the next. After a few days, the kids from the block came by.

"Is Wonnie still sick?" Jim asked my mom.

"No, but she's still recovering."

"Oh . . . Can she come out? Just for a little while?" Rachel asked.

Mom said yes, and off we all went.

"Let's go to the park," Rachel suggested.

"Let's ask Ericka to come along," I said. They all looked at me surprised.

"Ericka?"

"Yeah, she's cool. We're like friends now, you

know?" I said, like the fucking smug person I am. I bragged the same way I used to brag about a new toy or a new videogame.

Soon we tried to make Ericka part of our group. She laughed hearing Mark's lame horror stories, she went crazy with Rachel's total inability to catch a ball, she got us pumpkins to carve on Jim's patio, and she came along trick-or-treating on Halloween.

Sometimes Ericka did not want to do stuff with us.

We would be like, "Come on, say yes."

"I dunno, it sounds boring."

"Come *oooooon*, Ericka, come on."

She finally said, "Fine, I'll go."

I liked believing that she came because of me.

∗ ∗ ∗

Once Rebecca and I started dating, we became inseparable. Now, I sleep over at Rebecca's every weekend. We wake up late, have brunch somewhere downtown and then hang out at a park, a bookstore, or a coffee shop. Sometimes we just simply stay in, eat in bed, and watch TV. I like being with her. I like how she can be so easygoing. I like the warmth of her apartment. I absolutely hate her tons of pillows, but what can you do?

"Dude, you need an intervention. No one needs so many pillows."

"Oh, shut up! I might, just might, not need them, but they look so pretty, don't they? Come on, I know deep down under those baggy jeans and that fucking Phillies hat there's an understanding girl."

Fucking pillows, I hate them. But obviously tonight it's not the pillows that's keeping me up. It's the fucking idea of getting married.

Rebecca is right. Maybe under my clothes and my shaved head there is a girl, but this girl doesn't see herself getting married. Not now. This isn't an Ericka Gussen's let's-play-family kinda thing.

Rebecca actually sounded serious, though.

* * *

When I was a kid, winter was the worst. Not that we really cared about freezing our butts off on a typical Baltimore afternoon. The problem was that our parents cancelled our outside games. So we took turns playing at each other's houses.

Sometimes us girls played without the boys. Hours and hours with our Polly Pockets. But Rachel always wanted us to go with the boys and do something different.

"What you want is to be with Mark," Ericka would tell her.

"Yeah, you like him, don't you?" I would add, and then Rachel would throw a tantrum, saying that no, she didn't like him, that it was just too boring to play Polly Pockets all the time. Rachel simply stopped coming over. It was clear that it was all about Ericka and me. Ericka was mine and only mine. And I was hers.

Before Ericka, I never cared about my clothes. I wore whatever my mom got me. And my mom got me comfy clothes so I could play with my friends, and dresses for special occasions—though playing with my friends did not count as a special occasion. Then I noticed that Ericka was always cute, wearing matching outfits with bows or butterflies. I wanted cute clothes, too. No, I didn't want cute clothes; I wanted to *look* cute. Cute for Ericka.

"Why are you wearing that?" Mark would ask. "You can't play ninja with that."

"But she looks pretty," Ericka would add.

"Pretty? Ninjas aren't supposed to look *pretty*," Jim added. "Why are all of you all dressed up and wearing those shoes?" he said, pointing at Rachel's black Mary Janes. Rachel also wanted to stand out— for Mark, of course. Rachel and I always ended up changing into our "ninja" outfits, which was nothing more than sweatpants and a t-shirt. Not Ericka. She didn't like playing ninjas all that much.

"I'm off. No battles for me."

Once, we were all at Mark's without Ericka. Mark and Jim wanted to watch *The Incredible Hulk* for the hundredth time. I said, "No *Hulk*. Let's watch something else." Mark and I started fighting.

Mark was at his meanest. He was like, "It's *my* house and we are watching *Hulk*. If you don't like it you can just leave."

Then Rachel said, "Just go play dollies with your girlfriend."

I was like, "Shut up, you idiot." I left.

I was so mad. I was going home, but I knew that as soon as I walked in Mom would ask, "What happened?" There's no point in lying to Mom, she always has a way of getting the truth out of me. I knew she would say, "Go to Mark's and sort it out." Her saying has always been, "Friends are forever."

Anyway, I decided to go to Ericka's. She opened the door and I said, "I came to play with you, can we?" Ericka said yes with her eyes.

"I was watching *Raven*, but . . . we can play or something," she said turning the TV off.

"Don't turn it off. I like *That's so Raven*. Did you see that one when . . . "

"No, no TV. Let's play something."

Ericka already had her mind set. There was no point in arguing, so I said, "Okay, we can . . . we can play UNO?"

"UNO is more for a group."

"Oh, well, let's play with our Polly Pockets then, I can go get mine and . . . "

"No, we always do that. How about . . . how about we play Family?" It was a question, but it sounded more like a statement.

"Family?" I asked. "How?"

"Easy, come with me."

We were in her living room. Ericka pulled me by the hand into her mom's bedroom. She sat me down on the bed, opened her mom's closet and grabbed some shoes and a dress before saying, "You be the mom." She opened her mom's drawers, got a scarf and wrapped it around my head, then hung a pearl necklace on me. Any girl would have been thrilled to wear grown-up stuff. I wasn't that kind of girl. I wasn't into pumps and pearls and stuff. But if Ericka wanted me to do it, I sure would.

"Who are you going to be in our family?" I asked. Without giving me an answer she opened the other side of her mom's closet and pulled out a pair of men's shoes and a jacket.

"I'll be the dad."

Nothing seemed wrong with our game. I played along.

Since that day, playing Family became our favorite game.

Ericka's house became our stage. She always gave the instructions: "You are in the kitchen, cooking, and I arrive home from work, tired and upset." Yes, that sounded real.

"And how about I make your favorite dish and you bring me a present?" Yes, I wanted to be the co-producer of our play.

Ericka would add costumes and props to our fantasy and sometimes I would bring stuff from home for it, things I took from Mom or Dad. There were only two rules for Family. Rule Number 1: No one else could play with us. Rule Number 2: I would always be the wife and she would always play the husband.

She got an old briefcase. All the presents for me were hidden there. "Happy anniversary, Helen." Helen was my stage name. "Darling, I got you this, you have to wear it tonight." Next she would put a necklace or whatever on me and kiss my head. If it was a ring or a bracelet she would kiss the back of my hand. Just thinking about it gives me chills.

"Thank you, darling, you're spoiling me!" I'd say while ladling water from a pot to our soup bowls.

My "husband" and I would talk about our day over dinner. I would tell him about washing the windows, taking the kids to school, and arguing with the principal about the Spring Festival; and he would tell me about his grumpy old boss and how much he sold this month.

I have never thought of myself as a pretty girl, much less a feminine one, but back then, I was a princess: perfect hair and perfect dresses on my eight-year-old body. My husband? He was the most handsome guy in the world, I thought. The sweet, soft features of Ericka combined with her dad's clothes created a handsome masculinity.

I remember when her mom took us all to the air traffic control tower. We were super excited, so many buttons and shit. The boys and Rachel were asking questions and stuff. I wanted to ask questions, too, but Ericka was still in role, and as the guys in the tower explained their work, my husband whispered, "I love you," in my ear. No one noticed.

We forgot about everyone from the block that winter. When spring arrived, it was still all about us, all about our Family. I tried many times to be the husband. It made more sense: she was way more feminine than me. I could see myself in those pants and jackets. She would always say no.

"Rules are rules," she would say.

As Ericka and I played less and less with the kids outside, our games inside became more complex.

"Husbands and wives have sex, you know?" Ericka said one day.

Sex was not something I thought about all that much back then. I already knew what I needed to know: Dads stuck their penises in the moms' vaginas and after a few months, babies came along.

"But we can't have sex!" I told Ericka almost hysterically.

"I know, but we can have make-believe sex." I had no clue what she meant.

Our intercourse was knees on knees. Like spooning. First we rubbed each other's knees while moaning and making funny noises. Then we held each other for like the longest time. We had make-believe sex every single day.

My two favorite things in our game were dressing up in front of each other and going to bed. Yes, every day after dinner, my husband would take me to our room, which was Ericka's. My husband would take his shirt off and then take mine off. We would either lie next to each other on the bed or he would make me sit on the edge of the bed and start rubbing my knees. I got wet so easy. I didn't know what that was, but I did know it wasn't something I wanted to share. For a long time I used those memories of Ericka rubbing my knees or hugging me when I masturbated.

It was me who came up with the idea of grinding each others' va-jay-jays together, which Ericka liked better than our knee alternative. "This is more exciting, Wonnie!" she said. I probably experienced my first orgasm while playing Family.

Our game ended abruptly. My husband decided to abandon our family the day I got a mustache and asked her to kiss me with it on. I had found the mustache in our basement in a box with some old Halloween costumes.

I held the mustache above my lips with my fingers. "It still has the tape and you can stick it on and kiss me."

"Kiss you? Like where?"

I was firm and said, "Well, on the lips, dummy. Husbands kiss their wives on the lips, duh!"

"I dunno, Wonnie."

"If you want, I can wear it. I could be the husband from now on." That was my dream after all.

She went from a smile to a long line in her face.

"I don't know about that." And she left.

I went to her house the next day.

"Wanna play Family?" I asked. I had brought a plate of brownies. I also had the mustache. "We can celebrate our baby's birthday."

Ericka looked at me and said, "No, I don't. This game is boring now."

I got so upset. The game was *her* idea after all. I felt rejected. Still, I kept insisting.

"Come on, Ericka. You gotta. You be the husband." But she didn't wanna be my husband or my wife. She didn't want me, period.

I opened my mouth and said, "What is it, your dad never kissed your mom or you can't remember because he died so long ago?"

Ericka looked at me and pushed me away. I stood there, the mustache in my hands. I was about to leave when she said, "Gimme that."

Everything happened so fast. She snatched the mustache, removed the cover of the tape, and slapped it on her face. A second later, she pulled me to her face and kissed me. Ericka kissed me on the lips.

"There's your stupid kiss," she said. She pulled the mustache off, put it back in my hands, and said, "Now leave!"

I cried for days. My mom was worried. I didn't tell her what happened, but she could tell something was wrong. She probably thought this was just a girls' fight, and she encouraged me to go to Ericka's house to fix things.

"Friends are forever, Wonnie," she kept saying.

"Not this friend," I told her.

Ericka did not come to my ninth birthday party. Everyone from the block was there but her. "She's sick," someone said. I hated my party. We had cake and candies and a magician, but all I could think of was Ericka. Not even when my parents gave me my present was I able to forget about her.

"Look, baby, Dad got you a dog." Yes, on my ninth birthday, Dylan came to live with me, a furry friend to make up for what was to come.

The thing is, while I was playing Family next door, my parents were destroying ours. A month after Ericka Gussen's kiss and a week after our Fourth of July celebration and two days after my birthday, Mom and Dad told me they were splitting up. Our house was sold. Dad stayed in Baltimore because of his job. Mom was going back to nursing school and she wanted to go to Philadelphia so my aunts and my grandma could help take care of me.

"Take care of Dylan," Dad told me when we said goodbye.

Ericka and I did not speak to each other again. Ours was a different kind of divorce. I waved from the car to Mark, Jim, Rachel, and their moms, but Ericka was not there. I wished she had been out in front of her house. I wanted to see her one last time.

I wanted her to blow kisses to me. I wanted her to cry because of this new and definite separation.

My relationship with Ericka marked me somehow—not that I'm a lesbian because of her. She opened the door to something I didn't know I could like, or something I didn't know I already liked.

Now, years later, I've been asked to play Family for reals and I can't, I'm too young—I'm barely legal.

* * *

Fuck, the sun is already out. What time is it? Six thirty? Wow. I should just get my shit together and sneak out before Rebecca wakes up. I'll text later; I'll invent some shit. I don't wanna be here when she wakes up. I'm sure she'll rise with a strong desire to continue talking about *our* future.

Where are my sneakers? Oh, under that pillow. If we get married I will make sure we get rid of at least half of these pillows.

Did I just say *if*?

CHAPTER TWO

seven a.m.

"HEY WONNIE, WHAT CAN I GET YOU?" SAYS MISSY, the hottest barista in Thirteen.

"Can I have a caramel macchiato, no whip?

"Got it."

Café Thirteen will always be special for me. This is where I got my first job. This is where Fanny and I used to come. This is where Tori convinced me to make my *Come Out!* blog into a weekly podcast. This is where Fanny found me making out with Tori. This is where Fanny and I broke up. This is where I started dating Tori. This is where Tori sent me to hell. This is where I saw Rebecca for the first time.

"Caramel Macchiato, no whip."

"Excellent, thank you."

"You're welcome. Hey, is this your phone? It's vibrating," she says handing me my iPhone. I fucking leave it everywhere.

"It is. Thank you."

Dad. Damn it. Forgot to call him back yesterday. And the day before that. And the day before that.

"Hey, Dad."

"Hey, baby. You haven't returned my calls."

"Sorry, been busy." I hate that every time we talk on the phone I spend most of the time apologizing. "How have you been?"

"Missing you."

When he plays the victim I always strike back. "Oh, poor you. Follow me on Instagram. You will see me every day."

"Instagram? What's that? Everybody in the office talks about it." My dad is one of those dads who buys the latest in technology but has no clue how it works. "What's that noise?"

"Oh, it's a coffee grinder. I'm at a coffee shop. So, what's up? Why'd you call so early?"

"Ah, you know me—I'm an early bird. I see you are, too."

"Not really, I just fell out of bed." More like I ran out of bed.

"Wonnie, do you have any plans for the summer?"

"Why? You sending me to summer camp?"

"So you can kiss straight girls and get yourself in trouble again? No way!"

"She wasn't straight and it was a consensual kiss. And I didn't get in trouble. I've told you that a million times. Anyway, why are you asking?"

"I was thinking it's been a long time since we spent the Fourth of July and your birthday together, so maybe we could do something fun this year? Come and stay a few days. You can take a break."

My dad's name is Aaron Taylor. Grandma says that he wanted to be a lawyer ever since he was a kid. He wanted to be the kind of lawyer who would defend the poor victims of this unfair world. Civil rights and shit. My mom left nursing school and started working to help him accomplish his dream. The deal was that he would do the same for her later in life. He ended up being a corporate law attorney in this big company and my mom got tired of waiting for her turn to go to school and left. We left.

When I was a kid I thought Brown was the city my dad lived in. I believed he was like Mark's dad, who took the train Monday mornings to New York and came back on the weekends. Brown was not a city but the name of his firm, where he has spent more than twelve hours a day since I can remember.

"I can't leave everything just to have a few days off in Baltimore."

"Sure you can. Just figure it out."

My lesbian life started in a summer camp when I was eleven. Well, not my actual lesbian life, but that was when I realized I liked girls and only girls. I officially came out two years later. By then I had already kissed and made out with—one, two?—no, three girls. I have to thank my dad for that; he was the one who sent me to summer camp in Lancaster, Pennsylvania where it all happened.

When my parents divorced, I was supposed to spend summers with him. The first summer sucked ass because my dad's life was a mess. He was living the worst part of a bachelor's life. He was grumpy and had a smelly apartment without cable TV. When he found himself stuck with his pre-teen daughter for two months, he had no clue what to do with her. Hell, he didn't know what to do with himself.

But the next summer, he solved it: what do you do with a kid who likes running, jumping, climbing, and anything that involved mud and water? Summer camp, that's what you do.

Once we got there, he kept asking me, "Are you sure, Wonnie? Do you wanna stay, Wonnie? We can go back and figure it out. Maybe you can come to my office and . . . " I guess he was the one having second thoughts, but I wasn't. As soon as I got there, I loved it. My eyes found a great reason to stay. Oh yeah, a spectacular blonde instructor with the longest legs and the most beautiful face.

Miranda, eighteen years old, originally from California, but raised in the Amish Country of Pennsylvania. I had an immediate crush, although I didn't know it was a crush. Liking her didn't seem like a big deal to me, I just . . . liked her. Whatever she asked me to do, I would do it. I didn't know what I felt or that there was a name for it. Anyway, I would drool over Miranda and she probably liked the attention because she made me her assistant.

I was such a dork. Miranda no longer needed to take attendance or any other stupid chore; I was there for that. I was there to do all she needed, like a fucking servant. Before she finished sentences, such as, "Can anybody open the . . . " or "Can someone please put a . . . " I was there, right there, to solve it all. I just wanted to hear her say, "Thank you,

Wonnie." I just wanted her to caress my hair, kiss my forehead, or give me a bear hug.

One day, I had to take a fucking frog out of her cabin because she was afraid. (Don't ask me how she could work in a camp if she was afraid of a stupid frog.) She and the rest of the girls were freaking out. They were yelling, "Oh my God, it's there, right there! Get rid of it, Wonnie!" Then one of the boys started making fun of the whole situation.

"Look, the *tomboy* is saving the girls from a frog."

The tomboy, that's what they called me.

"You do it," Miranda told the kid. I gave him the stick I was using and decided to walk away.

"The tomboy is leaving," the boy said.

Miranda shut him up. Then she said, "Don't listen to them, Wonnie. I think you're cool and sweet and way better than any of those girls and boys. It doesn't matter, nothing matters."

It. She might as well have said, "It doesn't matter that you're a tomboy, nothing matters." I pushed her and ran to the lake and sat down on the dock.

When she found me she told me not to cry. She kissed me one, two, three times on my forehead and my cheeks. I thought I was going to die—her soft lips, her smell, her big blue eyes.

I liked her so bad.

In a way, I did know I was different, but hearing it, hearing the word *tomboy* felt like an insult.

"What exactly is a *tomboy?*" I asked her.

"A tomboy . . . a tomboy is a girl who acts like a boy.

"Oh."

"And sometimes, well, sometimes tomboys like only girls."

I understood it then. I was a tomboy. I acted like a boy. Plus I liked girls: I liked Miranda just as much as I had liked Ericka Gussen.

Tomboy or not, the girls at camp kept playing with me; I still liked singing and dancing to Avril Lavigne songs or pretending to be fashion models. Plus I was great at sports, so everyone wanted me on their team. *They* needed *me. I* didn't need *them.*

I was crying when my dad came to pick me up. His first words were, "Was it that bad?"

"No, I don't wanna leave. I'm gonna miss it. Will you bring me next year?"

"If you want to."

"Yes, I do, I do."

Just like I had found Miranda that summer, my dad found Jennifer. I did not like or dislike her, but I hated that he made a life after divorcing my mom. But Jennifer helped him get his shit together.

When I returned for my next summer in Baltimore, Dad had a different apartment, bigger, and most importantly, cleaner, and with cable.

"You sure you want to go back to summer camp?" he asked.

"Yes, Dad, yes."

"You can stay here and watch all the TV you want."

"Yeah, and Mom will kill us both, you know she hates me overdosing on TV."

"Summer camp it is then," he said. "But only for

a week this time. I'm planning to take some time off so we can hang out and . . . "

"No. I've been waiting *all* year for this," I said, when I actually meant, *I've been waiting all year for Miranda.*

Karma served me well, I think. My punishment for not wanting to hang out with Dad was that Miranda, beautiful Miranda, whom I had dreamed so much about, had moved to New York to try to be a model. I was disappointed but I survived. Some of the friends I had made the year before were there. I stayed at the camp for only ten days because I got my period. Yes, I got my stupid period and I totally freaked out and just wanted to go home.

The rest of my summer break I spent with Dad and Theresa, who had become his new "friend" after Jennifer broke up with him. Dad wanted to celebrate that I was not a kid anymore but a young lady, and he took us to the mall. He wanted to treat me by buying me a dress even though I said no like a million times.

"Come on, Wonnie. Why don't you just pick one?"

"I don't want to. I told ya I hate dresses. I hate them."

"But you used to like them."

"Not really."

I don't know how long we kept going at it, but at some point Theresa broke her silence, and said, "Aaron, if she doesn't want a dress, she doesn't want a dress. Not all girls are like *that*, you know?"

Dad didn't know. His argument was that all girls liked two things: dresses and making their parents' lives miserable. He ended up buying this fucking thing at Macy's. We were on our way to dinner when Dad stopped for gas.

Theresa reached back and touched my hand. "My dad used to do the same thing to me. He used to believe that if I didn't wear a dress I would turn into a tomboy."

Tomboy. There it was again, *that word.*

"But being a tomboy isn't bad, is it?" I asked.

"Mmhh . . . no, not at all. It's just, he doesn't get it."

Theresa was probably only trying to create a bond with me, but by saying, *They don't get it*, she made me understand something that by then I already knew. I was different and *he* didn't get it.

* * *

I've only been on the phone with my dad for three minutes when I interrupt, "Hey Dad, I'm sorry, I'm getting another call." It seems I'm always ending my dad's calls this way.

"Put it on hold. This guy at work just showed me how to do it on my phone . . . "

"Dad, I'll call you back as soon as . . . "

But Dad interrupted me. "Call them back. First, tell me, do you want to come? I can talk to your mom about it if you want me to."

"Dad, I'm not a little girl anymore. I'm 18. I can make decisions on my own. Fine, I'll go with you.

Maybe not two weeks, but at least a week." What did I just say? Dad just played his *I-can-talk-to-your-mom-about-it* card with me.

Fuck.

"You can bring Fanny if you want to," he added.

"Her name is Rebecca, Dad. How can you still confuse her with Fanny? It's been ages since Fanny and I . . ."

"Rebecca, I meant Rebecca, just bring her." He says goodbye and I'm left there thinking about Rebecca and me hanging out with Dad. I don't think so.

Fuck, Rebecca. I gotta text her:

Morning sunshine! I forgot I had this thing with my mom, had to run. See you at Candy tonite.

One minute. Two minutes. Three minutes. No reply. I guess she's still sleeping. Then:

Hey babe, why didn't u wake me up? I had Belgian waffles.

Meet before going to Candy, yes? We need to talk.

God, she wants to talk.

Rebecca started off as a rebound. I had just broken up with Tori who I had cheated on Fanny with . . . See, it's like this:

- Fanny: Girlfriend number one, met at summer camp.
- Fanny and Tori: Girlfriend number one and lover number one.
- Tori: Lover turned girlfriend for like a second, which in lesbian time means a month.
- Rebecca: Girlfriend number three came into my life when I wanted to show Tori that I wasn't a loser. Now my rebound wants to be my wife.

Oh, wait, I forgot to mention Heather, but things with her lasted less than a minute, which in lesbian time means two weeks.

There were a couple more girls that did not even last a second, which in lesbian time means a night or two.

Then Rebecca happened to me and I happened

to her. We've been together for more than two years.

But before Rebecca, before anyone else, Fanny was in my life. She's been my longest relationship.

Fanny, oh, Fanny.

* * *

I love summers in Philadelphia. It's hot and humid as shit, but there's so much movement on the streets. Tourists pointing at this building or that, tourists taking pictures, tourists eating cheesesteaks from sandwich carts.

I take what's left of my coffee, say goodbye to Missy, and walk out. I like people watching. I like imagining their lives, who they are, what they want. That dude over there for example. The one with the big camera, he left everything. He left his family, his home, and his job of the last fifteen years to become a photographer, until someone steals his camera and his wife will say, "Oh, that sucks, but you can go back to your job." Married life, man. We lesbians live relationships in a different way.

Different. Everything I do has to do with my *being different*, my being a lesbian. The books I read, the music I hear, the places I go, and the movies I watch. More than eighty percent of my friends are gay. Even my podcast has to do with this world.

Mom says that by doing so, I show no interest in diversity. I tell her that it isn't that I despise the straight world; I see her point, but at the same time I think this is important now. I'm still figuring out my own world, my *being different.*

Washington Square. Excellent. Let's find a spot for me and my computer. This is what I like the most about my job: I can do it anywhere I want. I'm a freelancer, managing social networks for different companies. Dad can't believe I get paid for simply posting stuff on Twitter, Facebook, and Tumblr. He says, "Come on, anyone can do that." In a way he's right, anyone can do it, but to do it well you need to really know your client and create an attractive online personality, and that's precisely what I do. Managing social networks is like writing a script for the screen: you wanna make it attractive, funny, sexy. Whatever it takes. Rebecca says that my job sounds like flirting. She's right. I help my clients flirt.

* * *

My *being different* became absolutely clear at my last summer camp, when I was thirteen. I started owning who I was. If I wanted to play rough with boys, I did. If I wanted to sing and dance with girls, I did. If I wanted to climb a tree, I did. If I wanted to spit, I did. Okay, maybe I didn't spit, but if I had wanted to, I would've.

Back to summer camp. That year, I felt too old for it, but Dad was working on some case that was gonna take all of his time. He suggested that if I wasn't going to go to summer camp, I could stay with his new girlfriend.

"You'll like Julie. I think she's the one. She has a

son almost your age. You can stay with them while I work."

"No, summer camp is okay," I said. I hated the idea of spending time with a new girlfriend and her son.

"Perfect," he smiled.

I'm glad I decided to go because I met Fanny.

"You are one bold girl," Fanny told me one night. We shared the same cabin and when you share the same cabin at a summer camp where they send you to sleep at eight o'clock, the thing you do is talk. We were talking about that day's activities.

"You're not afraid of anything," she added.

"Well, I'm afraid of bears."

"Well, yeah, but you're not afraid of anything else. I like that about you."

I started observing Fanny more and more. We spent the day together doing chores at the camp. We tried to be on the same team for competitions and stuff. I first liked her because she liked me, but then I liked her for who she was.

Fanny's long red hair, Fanny's freckles, Fanny's cute red lips. Yeah, I liked her.

We were walking to the river, only the two of us. Our hands and arms would touch from time to time until I decided to hold her hand. I noticed that I caught her by surprise; she stopped walking for like a second. Then she squeezed my hand.

We kissed for the first time that day. No tongue or anything, just a sweet kiss on the lips. I had finally gotten the kiss that I was craving from Ericka Gussen and from Miranda.

We got along okay with the other girls at camp, but we didn't fit in, either. Some girls complained about every activity, some girls would blister just by looking at the ropes, and there were some that were late for breakfast because they had been doing each other's hair. Not Fanny and me: we were the first ones to arrive for breakfast, the first to finish any kind of challenge, and the first to be picked for competitions. Fanny was fast; I was strong.

I was barely a teenager, but I had no doubt that

I liked her. She liked me too. Whenever the instructors weren't around, we'd hold hands or caress each other's hair. Once, we were on the dock with our feet in the river, her head on my shoulder, my hand on her thigh. Some kids walked by singing, "Fanny and Wonnie, sitting in a tree, K-I-S-S-I-N-G."

I could feel my face burning. I didn't know what to do. What was worse, I didn't know what Fanny was going to do. I thought she was gonna stand up, leave, and never talk to me again. Fanny did stand up but she did not leave. Instead, her right hand tightened into a fist and she yelled, "It's not any of your F-U-C-K-I-N-G business what we do."

So I stood up with her and said, "Get the hell out of here or we'll kick your butts to the moon." Okay, I probably didn't say all that, but I know I stood by her side and stayed there till they left.

No one messed with us again. They thought of us as an item. From then on they would say, "I'll take Fanny and Wonnie for my team."

We didn't know what we were doing. We didn't

know if girls could or could not be together like a boyfriend-girlfriend kind of thing, but that did not stop us. *I love you* was the last thing we said to each other when summer camp was over. Saying good-bye wasn't hard. We lived in the same city so we exchanged numbers and addresses. We promised to meet up. My last year of middle school was about to start and I wasn't the same old Wonnie because I had a girlfriend.

Like a typical teenager, Fanny wanted to have long conversations on the phone. Me? Not so much. I mean, I wanted to see her and talk to her, but to be on the phone for hours wasn't my thing. After a few weeks, right after school started, she decided we had to meet, hang out or something. Yeah, Fanny pretty much called the shots. She was bossy.

"Tell your mom to bring you to my house."

"I dunno."

"Don't you want to see me?"

"Yeah, yeah, I do." I did, I wanted to see her, and I wanted to hold her hand and touch her hair and kiss her all right. But my mom worked her ass off all day long and I couldn't see her finding the time to take me for a "play date." I told Fanny that.

"Play date, Wonnie?" she groaned. "We're not little girls. We don't do play dates."

"We don't, right. So what do we do?"

"We date, without the play in it. Listen, if you can't come then I'll visit you."

Because of her nursing school schedule, Mom sometimes couldn't do many things with me or for me. And when she started working in the hospital, she really couldn't hang out with me all that much. So it wasn't hard to convince her about me having a friend over while she was working.

Fanny's mom would drop her off on Fridays. We would watch TV, talk, or just simply spend the afternoon kissing. We went from sweet innocent kisses to French kissing and shit.

As I felt her tongue sliding against mine, I thought of Ericka Gussen. Fanny was not playing, she was for real and did not tell me to fuck off.

"What are we?" she asked me once.

"What do you mean?" I said.

"You and me, what are we? Friends?"

"Well, yeah. I mean, we're more than friends. You're more to me than anyone else at school."

"You know what a lesbian is?"

I didn't, but she did. Fanny explained to me what she had read in her mom's old edition of *Our Bodies, Ourselves*.

"So does that mean that we're . . . lebsians?" This is how dumb I was, I didn't even know my own category, but Fanny did.

"No, dork, the word is *lesbians*. And yes, we're lesbians. I'm your girlfriend and you're mine . . . "

I liked the sound of that. I sat closer to Fanny and gave her small kisses everywhere and then one long kiss on her lips. I have never kissed a guy, but I'm sure a guy's lips are not as soft as a girl's.

I had a girlfriend and I had to tell Mom. Why? Well, because Mom and I talked about everything and because I was happy. I liked what was happening to me and it seemed obvious that I had to share it with her. "You can tell me everything," she said all the time. And *everything* at that moment in my life was Fanny.

* * *

One night, after Mom and I dropped off Fanny at her house, I started The Conversation.

"Mom, do you like Fanny?"

"Well, yeah, she's very nice, isn't she?"

"Yeah," I said, "I like her a *lot.*"

"That's nice. As I always tell you, friends are forever," she said.

"Yeah, but she's more than a good friend."

"Hhmm?"

"Mom, she's more . . . She's more like my girlfriend," I said, looking at her while she drove.

"Well, yes, she *is* your girl friend. She's your best friend, isn't she?"

"No, mom, you don't get it. Fanny is my *girlfriend*."

We were already home. Mom was trying to park the car. What was normally a three-point parking job this time took her like ten. She was going back and forth, back and forth, the wheel steering one way, then the other. I could see her mind steering too. All of a sudden she stopped. She looked at me and asked, "Wonnie, what are you trying to tell me?"

"Promise to not get mad?"

"Promise."

"I'm in love with Fanny. We're lesbians."

"You don't know what you're saying," she said while turning off the car and getting her purse.

I stopped her. I grabbed her hand and said, "Mom, I do. I love her. We kiss and all that."

She looked at me. Her eyes went from anger to sadness to something I still cannot describe. Her voice cracked as she said, "Let's go inside. We'll talk about this some other time."

* * *

My mom's name is Winona, which is my name, too,
only nobody calls me that, except for Tori. I have
been Wonnie for as long as I remember. Mom works
at the Children's Hospital of Philadelphia. She's a
nurse and a certified midwife. She was twenty when
she met dad; they got married a year later. Both
of my parents dreamed of changing the world. My
dad would make justice for those in need and my
mom would be a nurse somewhere in a community
clinic. Then I came along and their plans changed
a bit. Well, no, my mom made her dream come
true, she does work in a hospital and every couple
of days she volunteers at this community center in
downtown Philly.

My mom is a nerd. She likes reading a lot. She
likes researching and learning new stuff. That's precisely what she did after I told her I was a lesbian.
She researched, talked to her colleagues, and even

had a session with one of the hospital's therapists. A few days after I told her I was a lesbian, she called me and told me not to defrost what she had left for dinner, "I'm picking you up in an hour. We are eating out, you and me."

"On a weeknight? Are you serious?" My mom would never let me eat out on a weeknight unless it was a special occasion.

The occasion was special, you betcha.

"So is Fanny the first girl you've liked?" Boom, she asked just like that as soon as we ordered our food.

"Yes. No. Yes."

"Yes? No? Which is more accurate?"

"I liked another girl before."

"Ericka Gussen, right?" It was shocking that my mom had thought of Ericka Gussen.

"No. I mean, I liked her, just not like *that*."

"Are you sure?"

I wasn't, I had liked Ericka Gussen like *that*, only I was too young to know it.

"There was this other girl at summer camp. Miranda. Only she was way older than me and . . . "

"What do you mean older? How much older than you? Did she touch you? Wonnie, tell me, did she *touch you?*"

"Mom, cut it out. No, she didn't. Nothing like that. She didn't care about me all that much."

"Did she make you do things?"

"No, Mom. Arrghh. No one did anything to me."

"Are you sure?"

"Yes."

Mom looked at me for like an eternity, the same way she still does to see if I'm lying or not. Then she went, "How did you know you liked Fanny?"

"I dunno, I just did."

"What do you like about her?"

I started telling her about the things we both liked. I told her about our long conversations about life and classmates and teachers. I told her how much I liked Fanny's crooked teeth and freckles. "It's like someone sprinkled paint on her face."

My mom laughed. I guess she just wanted to know if what I was feeling was real.

"Well, I think you two are too young to have a relationship, and not just with each other, in general . . . even with a boy. Relationships are hard. But if you are happy, then I'm happy." Then, after a long pause she went, "Just one thing . . . have you talked to anybody else about this?"

"No, why? What is it?"

"Nothing. It's just that sometimes people do not understand that *love is love.*"

My mom's words were beautiful, but, really, I had no clue what she meant until I came out to my friends at school and a few of them showed me nothing but disgust. When I told my mom about this, she simply said, "Well, fuck them." By then my mom was already going to meetings at PLGBTT: Parents of Lesbian, Gay, Bisexual and Trans Teens.

Fanny's mom was not so cool about this. She told Fanny what many parents of teenage kids say:

"You're just confused." And, of course: "You're doing this just to upset me."

But Fanny has the biggest balls on earth and she tried to stand up to her mom, and, when this didn't work, we decided to ask for help. My mom, a.k.a., Winona the Nurse, came to the rescue. She helped Fanny's mom to understand, accept, and acknowledge the importance of their support.

Fanny and I were openly together for almost three years. We had plans to travel to South America, backpack in Europe, move to L.A. for college, but then . . . then I met Tori and ended up cheating on Fanny.

So if my first divorce was with Ericka Gussen, Fanny was my second.

Am I ready for a new marriage? There is only one person who can help me figure this out. I hope she's up.

CHAPTER THREE
nine thirty a.m.

"Hello?"

"Hey, Mom!"

"Hey stranger, long time no see."

"Ha ha, I know, I know. Hey, what are you up to?"

"Not much, just came back from my morning walk. Where are you?"

"I'm at Washington Square, working."

"Office hours?"

"Yup."

"You're crazy . . . Hey Wonnie, Dylan has been being weird. I think he's getting sick."

"Why?"

"I don't know, he's been lazier than usual, haven't you noticed?"

"Not really, no. Have you talked to the vet?"

"Yeah, I was about to do that. Anyway, what are you up to? Am I seeing you this weekend or are you staying with Rebecca?"

I have two homes—sorta. I live with my mom. All my friends tell me I should be independent by now, but I like it there. I have a great relationship with my mom. Plus, it's cheaper than an apartment.

I also kinda live with Rebecca. I spend most weekends at her place. I come and go as I please. It's a bit of a mess too, but it's worked so far.

"No, I'm not staying with her. She's got . . . she's got stuff and . . . "

"Did you girls fight?"

"No, Mom. It's just, we both had things to do and . . . Hey, have you had breakfast?"

"Yes, tea and toast."

"That's barely breakfast. You wanna have something with me?

"Ummm, well . . . I'm a bit hungry again."

"Is that a yes?"

"Where do you want to go?"

"Wanna meet at Lula's?" Lula's is Mom's favorite restaurant and it's close to the park.

"Lula's, now?"

"Yeah, come on. It's Saturday, they have brunch. My treat. You know you want to, mmm mmm!"

"I can never say no to brunch. Fine, I'll just take a quick shower. Be there in a bit."

"Perfect."

"Okay."

"Mom?"

"Yes?"

"Call the vet. Make an appointment."

"I know, I know."

"And don't tell Dylan."

"Ha ha. I won't."

Mom talks to the dog as if he were a person. "You hungry? How about some biscuits?" or "Hey Dylan, tell Wonnie to rinse her plates after eating."

Passive-agressiveness through a dog, I call it. I wonder what's wrong with him. He was just fine a few days ago.

If I marry Rebecca, I wonder if she would want us to get a pet and be like those lesbians in Washington Square Park who walk three dogs apiece and talk about them, and *to* them, as if they were their kids. Would she want kids? Do I want kids? *Fuck.*

"You won't believe who I ran into yesterday," Mom says. "Oh my god, Wonnie, you have to try this. It's delicious. I had forgotten how much I like eating here."

This is her third cup of coffee, and her mood can now be described in one word: *crazy*. My mom is super-sensitive to things like caffeine and sugar. It's like she's high. "Oh, so as I was saying, who do you think I ran into?"

I give her a *no-clue* look.

"Emily. Emily Gussen! Ericka's mom."

What the fuck? Ericka Gussen's mom? Really? I must have a *what-the-fuck-are-you-talking-about* look now because my mom asks me, "Wonnie, you okay?"

I snap out of it. "Yeah, yeah, it's just the surprise. I hadn't thought of her . . . them . . . in—"

"In ages, right?" Mom interrupts.

According to my mom, Ericka's mom has lived in Philly for two years now. "She works for PHL, where she has a very important position. She's engaged—yes, engaged! She and her fiancée will get married next summer. They met when . . . "

As my mom goes on and on about Mrs. Gussen's love story, I'm dying inside. I want to know what has become of Ericka, A.K.A. my ex-husband. My mom's long story about Mrs. Gussen gives me time to create some possibilities. A) Ericka got pregnant at fifteen and she now has three kids and lives in the suburbs of Baltimore. B) Ericka is an environmental activist in New York and thinks of me all the freaking time.

C) Ericka ran away and joined a commune in Ohio where she's in charge of tomatoes and sheep.

"Oh, and she asked me about you."

"Mrs. Gussen?"

"No, weren't you listening? Ericka. Ericka asked me about you."

"Ericka was there, too?"

"Oh my God, Wonnie! Do you ever actually listen when I talk?"

"It's the coffee. You should've held off on that third cup. You're talking too fast." I move her cup of coffee away. She moves it back. I continue, "Now tell me all about it again. Tell me about Ericka. What does she do? What did you tell her about me?" My plan to sit down and open up with my mom fails. Her news is too juicy.

Ericka *fucking* Gussen has been living in this same city for two years now and I didn't know. She's going to Temple University, she wants to become a social worker, and she's single.

"I told Ericka you're taking a year off from

college. I told her about your freelancing, about Rebecca—oh, and the event at Candy."

"Wait, what? You what?"

That's the one problem of having a mom so involved in the LGBT community: she knows everything and persuades everyone to be involved in the "rainbow" movement, as she calls it. I'm not surprised she told Ericka about our benefit at Candy.

It was Mom who made me a "rainbow" girl. Mom got me involved with The Basement, which is a center created for lesbian, gay, and trans kids who need help. They provide counseling, workshops, and sponsor events and activities for our community. It's the best place to seek help if you live in Philly.

The first time I visited The Basement was right after Fanny left on an exchange program for one whole semester, and I was slowly dying. She wanted us to take a break.

"A break?" I asked her.

"Yeah, I mean, I know you love me. You know I love you. What's the big deal? Many queer couples have open relationships."

"An open relationship. That's what you want?"

"Unless you're afraid or something."

"Afraid of what?"

"I dunno, losing me? Ha ha. Don't make that face, silly." And then Fanny kissed me the way she always did: starting softly on my left ear, then my cheek, one, two, three kisses, and then the cherry on top—her tongue softly caressing my lips until it found its way to my mouth. When it came to kissing, Fanny was the best.

I gave in, but I had my doubts.

When Fanny left, I was kind of lost. I was sad. I was the bluest blue on planet earth. We were kids when we started dating. We had stopped trick-or-treating with the kids on the block three seconds before we became a couple. We were each other's first. We were the only lesbians we knew. So not only was I missing my girlfriend, but I was also missing my friend, the only person who understood me.

Winona the Nurse came to the rescue.

"You know, there's this place called The Basement. Have you heard of it?"

"The Basement?"

"Yeah, I can't believe you don't know about it. I got this brochure the other day. Look."

"And what's this Basement about?"

"They have meetings and workshops and social activities for teens like you, teens trying to . . . "

"Trying to what?" I asked.

"Trying to find friends who share the same interests," she said, smiling.

"And what are my interests, Mom? Please enlighten me."

"You know what? If you don't want to cooperate, just don't. I'm only trying to stop you from killing yourself with the Nutella you've been eating since Fanny left." She got upset and walked out of the living room—not without leaving the brochure on the coffee table and saying, "Please clean up this mess. I'm tired of doing—"

"—everything around here. I know, I know."

I took mom's brochure and read about The Basement. Maybe it wasn't a bad idea to try it.

My friends from school—Samuel, Jane, and Junior—were straight. The understanding kind of straight . . . sorta. Coming out to them wasn't that big of a deal, and although we got along, went out, had fun, worked together on school projects and shit, I felt something was missing between us.

I'd always tried to be involved in their stuff. I knew about their crushes and who they'd made out with. But they never asked about me and my love life. They would say, "Hey, how's Fanny?" or "Is Fanny going to the movies with us this weekend?" But that was it. It was okay to have a lesbian friend as long as they didn't have to hear about it.

Unless it was shitty stuff, you know. Bitching about girls was fine for Junior and Sam, they wouldn't mind that. Jane's favorite thing in the world was to experiment with my appearance. She would do makeovers on me all the fucking time. I let her because, whatever, but I never ever went out after her hands had been on my face.

I had friends, but at the same time, I didn't. So a couple days later, I went to The Basement.

My first time at The Basement was like going to the dentist: you really don't want to be there and at the same time you just want to get over with it. "Hi," I said to the girl at the counter. "My name is Wonnie and I'm a lesbian." Yup, that's what I said. The girl had half of her head shaved and the other half was long and curly.

She smiled at me. "Hi, Wonnie, welcome aboard. I'm Sonia. I take it this is your first time here?"

"Yup."

"And what can we do for you?"

"I . . . I don't know . . . A friend suggested I check it out."

"Well, first of all, congratulations on taking the first step. Are you out?"

"Out? Out of what?"

"I mean, have you come out with your friends and family? It's okay if you haven't, it's just something we ask . . . "

"Oh, yeah, yeah. I'm out, I just . . . " It was so pathetic. My stomach still hurts when I think of my first conversation with Sonia. "I don't know anyone like me, all my friends are . . . "

"Straight?"

"Yeah, I mean, they're cool and all . . . "

"Well, sure they are. There's nothing wrong with being straight. But if you ask me, it's kind of boring." I didn't know what to say. "I'm just joking," she added. "Look, Wonnie, you arrived at the perfect time. There's a group meeting in fifteen minutes."

* * *

"Wonnie, Wonnie, hello?" My mom brings me back

to reality. "I hate it when you space out, did you hear me about Ericka Gussen?"

"Yes, I heard you," I say.

"Do you want her phone number? I think I wrote it somewhere . . . "

"No, it's okay." I look at my mom's plate and ask her, "Are you done with that?"

"My God, you're hungry, eh? Does Rebecca feed you or what?" My mom exchanges plates with me.

"She does, it's only that . . . "

"Is everything okay, Winona? Is there something you want to talk about? Is that why you wanted to meet?"

"Can't a daughter just want to hang out with her mom?"

"Not really. Statistics say that relationships between mothers and daughters do not run smoothly until there are grandchildren involved."

"Mom, enough *Psychology Today*." Mom ignores my comment and simply asks for the check. Then she takes the fork out of my hand and asks, "So?"

"So what? Fork that over, man. You left half your food."

"What's going on?"

"Nothing."

"Does this have something to do with your father?"

"What'd you mean? I thought you guys didn't talk anymore."

"We do. He called me yesterday asking for you. He's been calling you and you don't pick up the phone. Winona, he's your father."

"Relax, Mom. I already talked to him this morning," I say, taking the fork out of her hand. "He wants me to take some days off to be with them and spend Fourth of July over there."

"Oh." The waiter brings the check, and after wrestling with my mom about it, I'm able to take it.

"I told you it was my treat," I say, and she smiles.

"You are such a gentleman," she says.

"Very funny. Hey, I was planning to go to The Basement, but I think I'd better go home."

"Great, you can come with me to take Dylan to the vet."

"Do I have to? I didn't sleep all that much last night and . . . ," I start saying.

"Shhhhh, spare me the details, please. You're coming with me. It's not like you do that much around the house."

"Here we go again . . . " I clear my throat and imitate my mom's old saying, "Wonnie, I'm tired of doing *everything*."

"Very funny, Winona, very funny."

As my mom and I walk to the car, she tells me about Dylan's symptoms and I can't find a chance to talk to her about what I actually want to talk about. Plus, there is a new issue on my table, Ericka Gussen.

Ericka. I wonder how she looks now.

CHAPTER FOUR
eleven thirty a.m.

DYLAN HAS BEEN THE ONLY PET IN OUR FAMILY pre- and post-divorce. I believed my parents when they said they got him for my birthday, but they actually got him to shield me from the drama that was about to come.

I love him, but my mom *adores* him. "I had a long shift and haven't been home. Dylan resents that." My aunts, her sisters, hate our dog; they say he is worse than a husband. "You just don't know him that well," my mom tells them.

After the divorce, Mom didn't do all that crazy dating that my dad did. When she finished nursing school, she went on a couple dates, but nothing happened. She lost interest. She'd say she wasn't looking for a relationship. "I have it all already," she'd say. "A fulfilling job, a daughter, and a dog."

But two years ago she met this physical therapist at the hospital. His name is George. Divorced, two kids. They dated for little over a year, though my mom always referred to him as her "friend" George.

They looked great together; Mom had never looked happier. Rebecca and I believed that at some point he'd move in with my mom and me because he was around our place all the time, but it didn't happen. I still don't know exactly what went wrong, but I remember one day I asked her, "Hey, how's George? I haven't seen him lately."

She looked at me and said, "And you won't see him around again."

"Why, what happened? Are you okay?"

"No, I'm not. I'm too old for this shit. Please, let's just pretend George never happened." Case closed.

* * *

Like every woman after a break up, my mom has good days and bad days. Today is a good day, maybe because it's Saturday or maybe because we ate at Lula's. Who knows? She left her hermit cave and now she's back to singing while driving.

Mom's like a teenager when it comes to music. She plays it loud. You turn down the volume and she goes apeshit. I'll do it once in a while just to mess with her. Right now, we're listening to REM's "It's the End of the World as We Know It."

"I've never understood these lyrics," I say.

"What?"

I turn down the volume so she can hear me.

"I said, I've never understood the lyrics of this song."

"Well, it's a song about everything. About change," she says before starting in again with the chorus. She turns up the volume. She bangs on the steering wheel every once in a while.

"I need to talk to you," I say. She can't hear me.

I could turn down the volume again and tell

her that Rebecca wants to get married and I have no fucking clue what to do. But I don't. I don't because she looks so radiant and happy and I like seeing her like that. I like my mom. She's just great.

The song ends. She turns off the radio and looks at me. "I need to tell you something," she says. She sounds serious. "I've been going to this group."

"What kind of group?" I ask her.

"A support group. I . . . I haven't been feeling well . . . "

"Because of George?"

"No. Well, yes, because of George, but not only because of George. I thought I was sad, but it's more than that. It's more than George. I'm turning forty this year and . . . "

"Come on, Mom, forty is the new thirty."

"I'm serious, Wonnie. I feel alone. You're with Rebecca most of the time, and believe me I'm not complaining. It's your life. I expect you to leave at some point and . . . "

"Geez, that sounds very loving."

"Wonnie, I'm serious. It's been heavy for me."

"What are you talking about? Don't you always say you have it all? A job that you love, your volunteering, your family . . . "

"Yes, yes. But at the end of the day, it's just me. So I started going to this place, and it's been really helpful. It made me realize that . . . " We arrive at the house. My telephone rings. I can't find it. It's hidden somewhere in my backpack. When I find it, it stops ringing. It was Rebecca. I silence it but my mom asks me, "Who was that?"

"Rebecca. No worries, I can call her later. Continue with your story . . . "

"Call her, I'll go get Dylan so we take him to the vet," Mom says.

I start dialing Rebecca's number. But then decide to just text her:

Hey babe, what's up?

* * *

Rebecca and I met at The Basement. It's located in the heart of The Gayborhood in Philadelphia, created almost twenty years ago by a lesbian couple, Ginger and Rose, who wanted to create an after-school support group for LGBTQ youth. Little by little, with financial support form other LGBTQ organizations, it became what it is today: A home for us queers.

When Sonia, the girl who greeted me on my first day at The Basement, invited me to stay for their group meeting, I expected a group where boys and girls my age would be crying about not being accepted by their relatives and being bullied at school. I expected drama and shit. I mean, I knew I'd been lucky with my mom and dad and aunts accepting me for who I was, and I felt lucky to have Fanny in my life, but I wasn't blind to what other teenagers like me had to go through. I felt I didn't have the stomach to hear sad stories, but neither did I have the balls to walk out.

I went into the room—a circular space with

colorful mattresses and cushions on the floor—found a spot and sat down. A few minutes later, a beautiful brunette girl sat next to me. She was wearing an old Madonna T-shirt, jeans, Converse, and had a huge flower tattoo on her left arm.

"Hi, I haven't seen you around. You new?"

"Ah, yes. First day."

"Welcome. What's your name?"

"Winona, but everybody calls me Wonnie."

"Winona is a great name, dude. My name is Victoria but everyone calls me Tori. You can call me whatever you want. Welcome to The Basement." Tori was wearing the most delicious perfume. I couldn't help saying, "That's a kick-ass tattoo."

"Thanks. Do you have any?"

"Tattoos? No. My mom would kill me. She's a nurse."

"Well, my dad did try to kill me when I had it done, but I had my mom's approval. How old are you, Wonnie?"

"Sixteen."

"Wow, you look like you're fourteen."

"Yeah, everybody tells me that. My girlfriend says that it's because I'm short and look like a hobbit."

"How's that?"

"Well, cute and shaggy."

"Ha ha, I think hobbits are far from being shaggy."

"Well, I'm from a different Shire."

I didn't notice then, but weeks later, Tori told me I was totally flirting with her that day. I think *she* was totally flirting with me that day.

We exchanged emails and numbers. I met her a couple times at The Basement. She was the one who took me to Café Thirteen for the first time, and to all the bookstores, bistros, and coffee shops around The Gayborhood. You could say that Tori was the one who introduced me to The Gayborhood. She became my mentor.

She also became the second woman I had sex with, and the reason Fanny broke up with me.

∗ ∗ ∗

Rebecca texts me back:

I miss u. How's your day going?

I'm with Winona the Nurse, we're taking Dylan to the vet.

What's wrong with Dylan?

Dunno.

Hope he's OK. Wanna meet before Candy? We can have an early dinner and talk . . .

Gotta call you later. Mom needs a hand with Dylan.

Great, now I'm using my mom *and* my dog to lie to my girlfriend. What am I doing? Rebecca isn't stupid; she probably knows I'm acting weird because of our conversation last night. I wish I could disappear for a couple days to figure things out.

She wants to continue our conversation today. Today. What am I going to say?

"Yes, Rebecca, let's get married and have a million babies," or "No, Rebecca, I'm not marriage material." How do straight people do this?

Here comes Mom.

"Everything okay with Rebecca?" she asks.

"Yeah. Hey Dylan. What's up, dude?" Dylan does look sick, now I kinda feel bad that I didn't want to come. Worse that I don't hang out with him anymore.

"You see his eyes? He looks sad, doesn't he?" Mom asks me.

"Yeah, a little. Has he been eating well?"

"Now that you mention it, not really."

"Well, he's old. Even old people eat less. Look at grandma. She eats one wing and half a cup of soup and she's full."

"Dylan is not like grandma."

"I'm just kidding."

"By the way, have you called her lately? She's been asking about you. Wonnie, I understand that you're older now and you'd rather hang out with your friends and Rebecca than go to your family's reunions but . . . "

"Here we go . . . "

"Don't you, *Here-we-go* me. Be serious."

"I will call her later, I promise."

"You better. At least just to say hi. By the way, you didn't finish telling me about your dad."

"Well . . . "

"Well?

"He invited me to go to Baltimore for the summer."

* * *

After the divorce, my mom believed there was no place but Philadelphia for us. One, because this is the city where she was born and raised. And two, because my grandma and her sisters lived there. Only family can shelter you after a break up, I suppose. So after emptying our old house and saying goodbye to friends and neighbors, my mom and I U-Hauled our entire lives to Philadelphia. We put everything in storage and moved in with my grandma.

My grandma's place is a typical three-story row house on Spring Garden. She had been living alone since my grandfather died, which happened pretty much when I was born so I guess that having us around was both wonderful and horrible for her. And for my mom. For starters, she did not want to sleep in her old room.

"But I got it ready for you," Grandma said. "I thought Wonnie could sleep in your sisters' room, it's bigger and . . . "

"I appreciate it, Mom, but I'm sure Wonnie won't mind changing rooms with me. Right, Wonnie?"

I didn't care. No room, no place, no city was home to me but Baltimore.

"Whatever," I said.

"Winona, you've made her mad." Grandma said. I wasn't mad, but I was definitely not in the mood to make things easy. After all, she was the one who dragged me away from my life.

The first few weeks of adjustment were hard. First, I had two women bossing me around about not eating in my room or doing homework. Then, only Grandma was around. My mother was back in school and we didn't see her all that much. So, to keep me busy, Grandma took me around the city all the time. Museums, parks, the market, you name it.

Grandma has a car but she doesn't like driving. She's the reason I refuse to learn how to drive. She always says, "Why spend energy in driving yourself somewhere if you can walk or have a driver take you wherever you want to go?" We would walk or take buses all the time. Yeah, she's the reason I know this city like the back of my hand.

My dad would call me every other day and once a month he would take the train and spend the weekend with me. So things were going okay, but not for Mom. I mean, she had school and stuff and spent most of the day studying or doing homework, but when she wasn't, she looked sad. Terribly sad.

"Mom, your phone is vibrating," I say.

"Can you check who is calling?"

"It's Aunt Tala."

"Well, answer."

"Do I have to?"

"Wonnie, don't start."

"Hey, Tala!"

I have two aunts. Tala and Dakota. They are identical twins. If you see pictures of them when they were kids, there is no way to tell who is who. They are great, but they are hard to handle. They are younger than Mom. My grandfather was an anthropologist; he worked with a couple of Native American communities. He chose the names for my mom and my aunts. Grandpa wanted me to be named Shikoba, which means feather. My mom says I was way too chubby to be called Feather; my dad says that when he first saw me he just thought I should have my mom's name. My grandpa agreed because Winona actually means, "firstborn daughter."

Anyway, when I came out to my mom, she asked me if I was planning to come out to my aunts and Grandma.

"Well, I hadn't thought about that yet. Why?"

"Just wondering. You know your aunts love you."

"But . . . "

"But they're not like me; not as open as I am."

Mom was right. My aunts are not like her. They are great but they can be so, so, so annoying. It's like they get paid a dollar every time they open their mouths.

Mom planned it all. She invited my aunts for lunch without Grandma. She said it was best if we did it this way. I don't know why but I accepted. We were eating my mom's famous crab cakes. Mom suggested that I do it after lunch, over coffee. They were all talking about Mom's new volunteering and I zoned out for a while, but then I simply opened my mouth and said, "So, I think I'm gay."

"What are you talking about?" said Aunt Tala.

"She's saying that she thinks she's gay. That is what you are saying, Wonnie?" Aunt Dakota added.

Mom was killing me with her eyes.

"Yes, that's what I said." Both of them exchanged looks and continued eating.

Finally Aunt Tala said, "Wait, so are you gay or do you just think you're gay?"

"I'm gay."

"You're young, you are just confused. You . . . " I will spare you this conversation where my Aunt Dakota pretty much said the same shit all parents say when you first come out. It takes years to learn that it isn't because they don't love you, but because you're breaking an image they have formed of you. Some people do learn to see you as you are, and their love doesn't change. Sometimes it gets bigger because they're proud of you.

It took awhile for them to understand what I was trying to explain, but they finally do, and Aunt Dakota says, "But promise us you will still make your mom a grandmother."

"Whaaa?"

"What? Nowadays, plenty of lesbians are having

babies from sperm they buy," said Aunt Tala. "Right, Winona? You must see things like this at the hospital all the time."

We all ended up laughing. Everything had gone smooth, unbelievably smooth. As they were leaving, both hugged me. I think I saw tears in Aunt Tala's eyes and both told me they were proud of me, and if any girl broke my heart they'd be sure to kick her ass. Then, Aunt Dakota stopped at the door and I swear I could see the wheels turning in her head before she said, "What about sex?"

"Sex?" my mom asked. "What do you mean?" But my aunt had her eyes fixed on me.

Then Aunt Tala, who I guess can read her sister's mind, said, "I guess her question is, are you having sex with a girl?"

I had all eyes on me, waiting for a response. "Sex? Oh, no. Well, I'm not having sex right now, I . . . I haven't thought about it," I said.

"Good, you are too young for sex," my mom said before opening the door for my aunts.

I was lying. Of course I had thought about sex, and I knew Fanny had too. It was on our minds, we just didn't talk about it all that much. But, oh boy did we explore each other's bodies.

This one time we were at my place. Mom was home but she had had a long shift at the hospital so she was pretty much in a coma in her bedroom. Fanny and I were in the TV room watching a movie. As always, we were holding hands, my head on her shoulder, her head on mine. Then I made my move. I started drawing small flowers up and down her arm with my fingertips. I could see from the corner of my eye that she was smiling. Then I softly moved my hand to her thigh; she was wearing shorts so it really made things easier. I started drawing imaginary flowers with my fingertips, then just scribbling around, up and down, up and down. She closed her eyes. I walked my fingers towards her inner thigh. She knew what to do. She opened her legs just enough so I could continue my "art" on her skin. We had done the same so many times before. Only now, I wanted more. I needed more.

I moved around so I could use both hands. I started on her shoulder with my right hand and moved towards her back, caressing her body with my palm. My left hand was busy trying to slip beneath her shorts. I leaned on her neck; small kisses here and there. My heart was pounding. I could hear her breaths getting deeper and deeper. Then, a small moan escaped from her lips when I made it through her shorts into her . . . her other lips. She was soaking wet. So was I.

She opened her legs even more. First I moved my hand inside her blouse, then down to her waist, to her hips, and then to her ass. I didn't really know what I was doing; I was just being led by instinct. My instinct and my desire and my curiosity. I wanted her. I wanted her so bad.

"You should lay down," I whispered. Fanny turned to me and started kissing me while pushing my hand deeper between her legs.

When Fanny left, I went directly to my room. I didn't wash my hand, but lay down on my bed instead, one hand between my legs and the other one covering my face.

The next morning Mom asked me, "Did you girls have fun last night?

"Yeah."

"What did you do?"

"We . . . we watched a movie," I said.

* * *

"Aunt Tala wants to know if you are going to the movies with them tonight," I say, as I hold the phone away from my ear for a moment and talk to Mom.

"No, I'm not. Tell her that Dylan is sick."

"Mom says she can't. Dylan is sick and she's staying with him."

Aunt Tala wants me to tell Mom that she's

offended that she loves the dog more than she loves her sisters.

"Aunt Tala says that it seems that you love Dylan more than . . . "

"Tell her Dylan is less opinionated than the two of them."

I decide to get out of this Ya-Ya Sisterhood and hand the phone to my Mom so they can solve their shit on their own.

Oh, sisters. Sometimes I'm glad I never had one. Although, girlfriends are sometimes as annoying as sisters.

* * *

"I hate waiting rooms," Mom says as soon as the vet's assistant takes Dylan inside.

"Isn't that weird?" I ask her.

"What?"

"That you hate waiting rooms. Your patients

spend their lives in a room patiently waiting for you. And now that it's your turn to wait . . . "

"Oh, shut up Wonnie," she says. She sounds mad, so I guess I better go back to playing on my phone.

"Do you have to be on that stupid phone all the time?" Mom asks me.

"Whoa, what's gotten into you?" I say while silencing my phone and putting it back in my messenger bag. "I'm sure Dylan is going to be okay," I add.

But I'm lying. I actually don't think Dylan is going to be okay. He's nine years old, which in dog years is like eighty or something. My mom looks the other way. She looks like she's about to cry. I then remember that we didn't finish our conversation about her group, but what if talking about it makes her feel worse?

I love women and love being a lesbian but I bet men are way easier to handle. Dad is easy to handle.

Dad! That's something I can talk about with Mom to distract her.

"So, what do you think, Mom. Should I go with Dad?" I ask innocently.

Mom looks at me as if I have just insulted her.

"Wonnie, do whatever you want. I'm tired of being between you and your father. I'm tired of helping you decide everything in your life," she says firmly before standing up and going outside.

I see her through the window. She's asking a stranger for a cigarette. She quit ages ago. She must be really upset and my asking about my dad's offer just made things worse.

Mistakes. My ability to make mistakes has been essential to reinventing myself. I have made mistakes with everyone around me: Mom, Tori, Fanny. Especially with Fanny.

When she left for Germany, Fanny decided

we should have an open relationship so we could experience other people. I didn't like that idea, but I ended up saying yes. Big mistake. I should have said, "No, I don't want that." I should have been firm. But I wasn't. Once she got back, she said she missed me miserably and regretted our agreement.

"Let's not talk about what we did during this time. Let's pretend it didn't happen," she proposed.

"Let's," I said.

I kept my promise. Not once did I ask or mention anything about our time apart. But I made another huge mistake. I didn't break up with Tori.

It was a Saturday afternoon. I told Fanny I was going to be at The Basement and then hang out at Café Thirteen. I had invited her to both places many, many times, but she had always refused to go. I didn't insist all that much because it meant I wouldn't get to hang out with Tori. But that day Fanny changed her mind and surprised me at Thirteen. She was the one who ended up surprised when she found me making out with Tori.

"You are a fucking asshole!" she said and left.

That mistake forced me to reinvent myself. I became a new Wonnie. I became a fucking asshole, I guess. I started fooling around more and more with Tori and when things ended with her, too, I decided to show her I had moved on and started fooling around with this and that girl. Then, I met Rebecca who wanted a serious relationship and I stopped being a fucking asshole, at least for a while.

"I'm sorry to tell you that I don't have good news," the vet says.

"Wait," I tell him. "Let me call my mom." But Mom had just walked in.

"What is it? Just tell us," she says.

"Dylan has a huge lump on his stomach. I need to do a biopsy and have it analyzed, but with the symptoms you described, I'm afraid there is a good chance that . . . "

"It's cancer," finished Mom.

"Maybe, yes. I'm giving you the worst case scenario because I want you to be ready. I want to run some tests to be sure."

"Can't you do a surgery or something?" I ask.

But before the vet comes up with an answer Mom says, "Is it too advanced?"

"Can't tell. I would like him to stay here for observation. I have given him a sedative for now so he's not in pain. Go home. I'll call you as soon as I have news."

We stay in the car for a few minutes before Mom decides to turn the engine on.

She drives slowly. No music now. The two of us quiet. I can see tears running down her cheeks. Telling her about Rebecca's proposal is out of the question now.

When we arrive, Mom goes straight to her room and closes the door. It's one p.m. and I haven't recorded my podcast and have three missed calls from Rebecca.

CHAPTER FIVE
one p.m.

WILL TURN NINETEEN THIS SUMMER. AT NINETEEN YOU are supposed to be in college. You are supposed to be living on your own, leaving your hometown behind. But I'm not into that shit. Not yet. At some point in my senior year I said to my mom, "So, the school counselor wants me to fill out all these papers to apply for college . . . "

"And?"

"And I don't know if I want to."

"How so?"

"Well, I've been giving it some thought . . . "

"Yes?"

"Would it be really bad if I took some time off before actually going to college?"

"What about that Communication and Media program in New York?"

"You see, once I'm in school, classes are gonna take over my life. My freelancing, my podcast will have to be put on hold, and I want to enjoy it just a little longer. Plus, I . . . I know it sounds silly, but I'm not ready to leave Philadelphia."

My mom wasn't opposed to it; she just didn't get it. She told me for the twentieth time that when she was my age, she counted the days for high school to be over so she could pursue freedom.

"You are nothing like Grandma! I have always felt free living with you. I fly away every time I cross that door."

"And then you fly back and leave a mess."

"Mom, I'm serious."

"Well, if that's what you want, but, isn't it weird?"

"What?"

"That you would want to still live with me? Most of your friends are independent."

"I'm independent."

"Really? When was the last time you did your laundry or bought milk or dog food or . . . ?"

"I . . . I . . . Mom, what can I say? I like the way *you* do things."

"Don't try kissing my ass. You're too old for that. But I'm serious. All of your friends live on their own and if you stay one more year . . . "

"Or two."

"Or two?"

"Or forever," I said, forcing Mom into a hug.

"Oh, Wonnie. That would be sad."

∗ ∗ ∗

I like living with Mom. Not only does she make things easy for me—and my laundry—she also believes in what I do. See, I have always liked computers and shit, and I'm really good with them. It all started when I became part of the Radio Crew at my school. I was there just to help out with putting the booth together and before I knew it I was playing music and talking about the stories behind the songs, the stories behind the artists. "You should have your own show," someone suggested.

Back then Fanny and I would watch episodes of that Showtime series *Queer as Folk*. I was telling her about doing a radio show in my school and she said, "You should name it *Queer and Folk.*"

"Are you serious?"

"Totally."

That's how it all started. *Queer and Folk* was about me playing music by queer artists and talking about them. Before I realized it I was revealing stuff about myself. People in school freaked out—teachers, I mean. They didn't want a show about sex.

"That's not why we let you guys start a radio station at school." I was smart enough to defend myself: I explained it had nothing to do with sex but with diversity, with having an open mind.

They weren't convinced. So I had to play music and leave my opinion outside the booth. I couldn't go against school policy, but I felt I had too much to say. By then Fanny was in Germany and I was hanging out a lot at The Basement so I was learning more about my community and I wanted to share, music, ideas, experiences.

I was telling Tori about all this, and she said, "Well Winona, why don't you do a podcast?"

"A podcast?"

"Yeah, you created the web page for The Basement. That means you can create a link from it to your own website and upload weekly podcasts. We can all help you spread the word through Twitter, Facebook . . . "

A podcast sounded great to me.

"I'm gonna need to get more music and a mic and . . . "

I borrowed money from my dad. He seemed happy that I was relying on him and that I had this project.

I bought a microphone, headphones, and a bigger hard drive for my computer. I found myself a sound program so I could run my show even better. I moved things around in my bedroom so it could become my studio. I was so nervous.

I was trying to draft a script, but it was clear I had writer's block. So I decided to go to The Basement. Tori was going to be there all afternoon; she would definitely have ideas for me. When I arrived, everyone looked weird. Sonia and some other kids looked as if they had been crying.

"What's going on?" I asked.

Sonia looked at me and said, "It's Jimmy, Wonnie. Our beloved Jimmy."

Jimmy started going to The Basement almost at the same time as I did. Cool guy. We were each other's first gay friends. We had many things in common: we were both only children, our parents were divorced, and we were both very young when we realized who we were. There was one big difference between us, though; he hadn't come out to his family. Unlike Winona the Nurse, Jimmy's mom was a church lady who believed being gay was a disease. His dad was just an asshole.

Jimmy's dream was to become a writer, a poet. You would always see him with his little messenger bag full of books and notebooks. He'd take notes after hearing something or seeing something. "That's a beautiful image, hold on." Jimmy would say before taking his notebook out to write something down.

"What about Jimmy?" I asked Sonia.

"Well, he came out to his father, but . . ." Sonia was interrupted by her own crying. "But his father didn't take it well, and who knows what he told him. Anyway . . . Jimmy is dead."

"What the fuck—are you serious? What happened?"

"He hung himself."

"He *what?*" I couldn't believe it.

Tori came out of the bathroom just then. She too had been crying.

"No wonder he was so afraid to come out, so

afraid of his father. I can't even imagine what he could have told Jimmy for him to do *that*," Sonia added.

Jimmy's death had a huge effect on all of us. I remember that day I walked home from The Basement and all I could think was how lucky I was to have the parents I have. My mom had always been so supportive. It took longer for my dad to accept that his daughter, his little girl, was a lesbian, but not once did he give me a hard time. How is it possible that some parents can't understand that, as my mom says, *love is love?*

Jimmy's death made me rethink what I wanted to do. *Queer and Folk* disappeared from my mind and *Come Out!* was born. My podcast was going to reach others, share experiences, and everything I had learned from the crew at The Basement. Guests would narrate their coming-out stories.

It's been two years now. It feels nice to see my stats on the webpage and learn how many new visitors I have every week. I receive emails from kids all over Pennsylvania, kids who are like me. Kids who are figuring themselves out. It's because of my podcast that I want to do a BA in Media and Communication at NYU, and my podcast is also the reason I'm taking this year off. There's just so, so much that I still wanna do with it.

Preparing a show takes me two days. One day of writing, researching, looking for songs, checking email for questions and special requests. I write my own script. I take my podcast as seriously as I would a TV or radio show. I believe having a good compilation of my podcasts will become a nice port-folio for the future. Anyway, when I'm done with my script, I start my actual recording. I don't have the greatest equipment but so far, so good. The opening song of my podcast is "I Would Walk 500 Miles," that old song from The Proclaimers. It was Jimmy's favorite. I wanted my work to have some sort of Jimmy's print on it. I know he would have liked it.

* * *

"Today we will continue with last week's controversial topic: Bisexuality. People think that teens come out as bisexuals before actually admitting they are gay or lesbian. Is that true? Share your thoughts on my page. Cherry Pie, wherever you are, thanks for recommending *Look Both Ways: Bisexual Politics* by Jennifer Baumgardner. I will talk about this book and some things that I have learned from it. I also have a set of songs that explore bisexuality. Let's start with a country song, "My Wife Left Me for My Girlfriend" by The Bellamy Brothers. I'm Wonnie Taylor and this is *Come Out!*"

Little by little more people have started following the show through Twitter and I easily befriend ten to fifteen people on Facebook every day. When I'm doing the show I keep the Facebook chat open so people can ask questions, request songs, anything. Tori says that it is surprising I don't get too many weirdos asking me for erotic stories on the show. I've had a couple though, one person wanted me to share sex tips to make a girl come. I said, "If you have to ask that, then you will never make a girl come." I pissed him off because he told me his dick was way better that my dyke finger. I didn't reply. I simply unfriended him.

Last week I talked a bit about tonight's event at Candy's. We're doing a costume party to raise funds for The Basement so that they can start doing travelling workshops. The plan is to go to some community centers all over Pennsylvania to talk to kids about LGBT issues. Tori's been trying to convince me to come along. She says I'm a celebrity already and I could attract more people to our lectures. I don't know though. Rebecca's in charge of these workshops and we both like the idea of doing something like this. She says it would teach us both to be together 24/7.

I should call her. But what am I going to say? I wonder if Tori knows about Rebecca's proposal. They tell each other everything. Tori. I wonder if she's online . . .

I look her up on Whatsapp and send a quick message. Hey Dude...

She replies right away. Where you been? Thought you were coming to Candy this morning to help with decorations.

Got some stuff at home. You know, with Mom.

Oh, yeah, your dog right? Rebecca mentioned it.

Did she say anything else?

Nothing . . .

Nothing?

Nothing except that you fucking ran away from her place this morning before sunrise.

Shit. Just for the record, I didn't run away. I just left before she woke up!

U sure?

Yes. Did Rebecca really say that?

No, she didn't.

Asshole.

A big cute one. Hey, did I touch a nerve there?

What you mean?

You and Rebecca. What's going on?

Why? What did Rebecca tell you?

Well, she said you guys had a serious talk.

Ehm, yeah. Kinda. She wants to get married.

Shut the fuck up! You OK? Need to talk?

It's been a weird day. It seems like past, present, and future is right here, sitting on my lap.

What do you mean?

I don't wanna type all this shit. You busy?

Not really, just finished up at Candy. Do you want me to come over?

That'd be great.

OK, lemme take a shower because I'm sweating like a pig. Those fucking fairies had me setting up the longest line of lights on the ceiling.

You talking about Jeff and Daniel?

Yeah, they Martha Stewarted us all morning.

* * *

Victoria. Tori. She's twenty-two. She goes to UPenn. She's the fucking smartest woman I have ever met.

She's from Buffalo but her parents moved to Philly when she was ten. She's the youngest of four siblings. She grew up playing football and climbing trees with her brothers, but at the same time, she liked Barbies and dolls and girlie shit. Just like me. She says she knew she was gay when she was in middle school and could not stop checking out her English teacher's boobs. She says they were humongous.

She says that boobs were all she could think about. She could not help glancing at every pair of boobs that walked in front of her. Tori would watch movies with her brothers and the three of them would be doing the same thing, waiting for a girl to run and see those things bouncing.

It was actually her brothers who told Tori that maybe, just maybe, she was a lesbian. Tori asked them if that was bad. They said no, but recommended she not tell their parents, just in case. And she didn't, because just like me, she didn't know exactly what it meant to be lesbian. Tori only knew two things: she liked girls and she liked boobs.

I told Tori everything about me, about my games with Ericka Gussen, about Miranda, and about Fanny.

"Fanny sounds like a smart girl," said Tori after I explained to her about our open-relationship agreement.

"She is, but I don't know how I . . . "

"How old did you say you are?"

"Sixteen" I said.

"Well, there you go. At sixteen you are supposed to be exploring life and pussy."

"What?"

"Don't get me wrong. It's great you and Fanny found each other and shit, but . . . aren't you even a little curious?"

"Curious about what?"

"Pussy."

"I never call it that."

"What do you call it then? *Down there?*"

"No, no. I don't know. I don't call it."

"Rule Number One of the Lesbian World: we

call it *pussy*. Repeat after me: *pu-ssy*. We can spell it together if you want. P-U . . . "

"No."

"Come on, try it."

"I don't want to."

"How 'bout touching it then?" Tori said, pulling my hand and putting it between her legs.

"The fuck you doing? There's people here, Tori."

"Winona, nobody cares about what we do here." Tori pulled me towards her. She started kissing me. I tried to resist at first, but soon my tongue was exploring hers, my hands on her thighs, her hands on my face.

"Let's get out of here," she said.

Tori smells like jasmine. She's like a drug. Sex with Tori is great. Yeah, we sometimes still hook up. It doesn't mean anything. We have always been and will always be just friends, *special friends*. Her decision, not mine. Rebecca knows Tori was the reason Fanny broke up with me. She just doesn't know that from time to time Tori and I still have sex. It would kill her. Rebecca does not believe in open relationships *at all*.

I love Tori and she loves me, but we're not in love. Tori's the one who actually introduced me to Rebecca. I didn't pay much attention to her then. I was dating Tori. Correction, I thought I was dating Tori, but as she explained to me some time later, "We are just *special friends*. This isn't a relationship, are we clear?"

Blunt. I was torn apart. Fanny had broken up with me because she saw me with Tori. I was heart-broken but I thought, "At least now I have Tori." I was wrong.

The only thing left for me was to do was what Tori suggested: explore life and pussy. I went out with a couple of girls, kinda jumping from bed to bed.

Until I finally set my eyes on Rebecca. The truth is I asked her out, hoping that Tori would find out and make a big deal about it and realize she was losing me. Tori couldn't care less, and it was okay, my attention was all on Rebecca. What started as a rebound became something else.

Rebecca is unlike any girl I had met before. It's easy to fall for her.

* * *

"In *Look Both Ways*, Jennifer Baumgardner says that we have been looking at bisexuality the wrong way, making the identity entirely dependent on someone other than the bisexual person him—or herself. You are a woman dating a man. You are straight. You are a woman dating a woman. You are lesbian. It's not that easy, as she states on page six, 'Sexuality is not who you sleep with, it's who you are.' I will leave you all with that thought while we listen to 'Bisexual Girl' by Coyote Shivers."

I play the song and then hear the doorbell. I run downstairs and open the door. Tori.

"Wow, that was fast," I say.

"I didn't shower, thought I could do it here."
Tori was a mess, indeed.

"Sure. Let's go upstairs."

"Is Nurse Winona here?"

"Yeah, she's in her room."

"I haven't seen her in a while. How is she?"

"Can't tell, actually. Today we were talking about stuff, her stuff, but then this shit with Dylan . . . "

"What did the doctor say, anyway?"

"Cancer."

"Fuck."

"Yup."

"Are they going to put him to sleep?"

"Don't know yet."

"I'm sorry for your mom. She loves that furry thing, right?" Tori sits down on my bed and starts taking off her Doc Martens and her socks.

"Yeah, she does. Plus, she still hasn't gotten over the break up with George."

"Fuck."

"I don't know, man, my mom is being weird."

"She's not weird, she's just forty-something."

"I guess."

"So, tell me, what is this marriage thing Rebecca is talking about?" Tori asks as she starts taking off her jeans. She's wearing a thong. I hate those—I don't know how girls can put up with them.

"She wants us to be a family. She wants commitment," I explain to her while she takes the rest of her clothes off and grabs a towel. She goes to the shower but leaves the bathroom door open so we can talk.

"I always knew Rebecca was the marrying kind, but . . ."

"What do you mean?"

"Listen, I have no doubt Rebecca is a lesbian but I think she's a straight lesbian."

"Tori, you still on that?"

"You know I'm right. Rebs wants what a straight girl wants—a husband, kids, a home. The question here is, why does she want it now?"

"I don't know."

"Have you been a good girl?"

"A good girl?"

"Have you been fooling around, Winona Taylor?"

"No." Long, long pause. "No more than usual."

"Are you still doing Missy from the coffee shop?"

"Missy? How do you . . . ?"

"Oh, come on, dude, I wasn't born yesterday. I know you so well."

"It takes one to know one, right?"

"Shut up," Tori yells.

I check how long I've recorded, then pause my program.

"So, have you?" Tori sticks her head out of the shower to hear my answer. I can see her half-naked. I can see her big, brown, round nipples. They are gorgeous.

"No, not since she started dating that girl from the bookstore."

"What about that other chick, what's-her-name?"

"Who?"

"The one with the blueberry boobs."

"What does that even mean?"

"Small and perky."

"Oh, well I do like 'em small and perky," I laugh.

* * *

I like girls, I can't help it. I like how they smell. I like how they taste. I like the lines of a woman's body. I think I was born to spread love to the women around me. Tori says I'm a player. I am. I mean, I love my girlfriend. Rebecca is amazing. She's smart, she's brave, funny, sexy. I'm proud of her. But sometimes I need to spice up my life. I'm very careful. I don't want to hurt her, obviously. She still cries when she remembers that once I proposed we have an open relationship:

"Why would you want that? Aren't you happy with what we have?"

"I am, I'm very happy. But Rebecca, I'm your first girlfriend and I think it's healthy that you explore what's out there."

"Oh, so you're doing it for me? You wouldn't do anything with anybody else?"

"No. I don't know. Maybe. What I mean is, it's only fair that you see what is beyond us."

"Listen Wonnie, I'm very happy as we are. If you aren't, we can just leave things right here. I don't need to go eating pussy here and there to gain experience. I'm not Tori."

"What do you have against Tori?"

"It's not that I have anything against her. But she's a player and she's afraid of commitment. That's why she goes from girl to girl. That's not what I want. So, you are either in or we are off." Tori *is* a player, Rebecca is right, but I'm one, too, only my girlfriend doesn't know.

"Rebecca, baby, don't get mad. I'm sorry I even suggested it. I only wanna be with you. I'm not like Tori."

"Well, I'm not either. If we want this to work, we gotta be honest with each other."

"Yes, of course," I said, but I was lying. I haven't been all that honest, I know.

It's not like I bang every sweet piece of ass I see. I just happen to like fooling around once in a while, but that doesn't change the fact that I love Rebecca. I love her more than anything.

I happen to believe that you can be in bed with somebody else even when you are *in love* with someone. If *love is love*, then *body is just body*. It's socially accepted that men sleep around, so it can be the same for women. As long as no one gets hurt, of course.

I know it would sound odd to say that I want Rebecca to experiment with someone else once in a while, but I really think she should, and, no, it would not make me jealous because in the end it's me she loves, it's me she wants to be with. Being polyamorous isn't bad; at the end, what the word means is lots of love.

* * *

Tori comes out of the shower and pats her body to dry herself. She puts the towel around her hair and walks out of the shower naked. When I met her she only had one tattoo on her arm, now there are four of them all over her body. My favorite is the one in between her boobs. A monarch butterfly. Tori is so beautiful, I never get tired of seeing her. It's like she seduces you even without wanting to.

She pulls out her clothes from her bag and says, "You *know* who I'm talking about, that chick who reads the tarot on Washington Square on Sundays."

"You mean Susan."

"Susan, that's right. So, you are doing her too?"

"What's with all this questioning, Tori?"

"Susan's on the list, check." Tori stands in front of me, her undies are a mismatch, like always. She continues, "I think Rebecca smells that you're fucking around."

"Shut up."

"Listen, Wonnie," Tori rarely calls me Wonnie. She calls me Winona because she knows I hate it.

I tried doing the same, calling her Victoria, but I can't. It just doesn't feel natural.

Tori sits on my bed, right next to me. "I love you very much, but I also love Rebecca and I don't think you are being fair to her. She's in love with you."

"I love her too. I wouldn't hurt her."

"Oh, but you do. Every time you have sex with another girl, you hurt her."

"But that has nothing to do with love. Sex is sex," I approach her. I caress Tori's shoulder. Next, I walk my fingers up to her neck, the way she likes it. I get closer and smell her back.

Tori stands up. "Sex is never just sex, and you ain't getting any with me today," Tori says as she pulls on her jeans.

"Look who's talking? You're the Queen of Casual Sex."

Tori gives me the finger before saying, "Winona, she knows."

"She knows nothing. Unless—have you said anything to her?"

"No, you idiot. Of course not. I don't mean she *knows* knows. But I'm sure she knows. I'm sure something in her mind is telling her that you aren't completely committed to her. Girlfriends always know."

"You think maybe that's why she wants to get married?"

"I am *sure* that's why she wants to marry you."

"Fuck."

"Yeah, fuck."

"What am I going to do? I love Rebecca but . . ."

"You need to say no. You need to let her go."

"But I love her."

"Do you?"

* * *

Rebecca is what Tori calls The Cheerleader Type. She's the kind of girl that, according to Tori,

"Doesn't know she likes pussy until she eats pussy." She was purely straight. She dated a lot of boys, and if she hadn't met Sonia—yes, Sonia from The Basement—she'd be on her way to being married to her high school sweetheart.

She and Sonia weren't in love or anything like that. They met when Rebecca went to The Basement to get help for her younger brother, Vinny.

Vinny is gay and he was having a hard time dealing with it, plus he was being bullied all the time in school. Sonia walked her through The Basement and showed Rebecca the different programs available for her brother. Rebecca says she paid attention to every little thing Sonia said, but she could not help staring at her.

Rebecca is a sweet girl, yes, but she can be pretty straightforward. I mean if she wants something, she goes for it. Nothing stops her.

After a few times hanging out at The Basement, she asked Sonia out. Sonia said she couldn't date clients. But technically, Rebecca wasn't the client, so she kept asking until Sonia said yes. Again, theirs wasn't a relationship, but let's say that Sonia was her first.

Rebecca does not see herself as lesbian or bisexual. She says she's queer, period. I don't argue about it anymore.

Rebecca started volunteering at The Basement, and she met Tori who introduced her to the whole gang. I didn't pay her much attention when we met as I was still going through my Tori phase. Rebecca says that she was into me since she saw me; she knew I was "the one." She did everything she could to get my attention and win my love.

I wasn't all that into her at the beginning; I think I became closer with Vinny. But as she started opening up with me, I learned what a wonderful girl she was. She's smart, strong. She's an achiever. As I said, once something gets in her mind, she won't stop until she gets it. For example with Vinny, when Rebecca realized that her brother was going through hell at home, she decided it was time to stand up for him and give him the life he deserved.

See, when Vinny finally came out, her parents were mad. They tried to kick him out of the house. Rebecca said, "If he leaves, I leave and you will never see either of us again. So you can take your time to process this or you can say goodbye to us."

She has big balls.

There was a problem though; her parents refused to process anything.

* * *

"I can't just break up with her," I said to Tori, who was now fully dressed.

"Why not?"

"Because I love her. I like being with her. I like the idea of sharing projects with her at The Basement."

"Dude, it sounds like you are talking about a colleague not about *your* girlfriend."

"Shut up. It's not, you're not . . . "

"Wonnie, you need to talk to her."

"I can't."

"Then, commit. Commit to her."

"I'm committed."

"No, you're not."

"Oh, I don't know what to do, Tori!"

Tori stands up, puts her t-shirt on, and walks around my room. She finally sits down in front of my computer, as if it will give us an answer.

After a few minutes of looking at my screen she asks, "Who's Cherry Pie?"

"Who?"

"Cherry Pie, here on your website chat."

"Oh, I don't know. Someone who listens to my podcasts all the time."

"Cherry Pie has balls or pussy?"

"I don't know."

"Well, he/she wants to know if you are going to Candy tonight."

"What?"

"Seems you have a fan."

"Shut up."

"Or a stalker."

"Blow me," I say and reach over to turn off my screen.

"That ain't gonna happen," Tori says. "Anyway, what're you wearing tonight?"

"I was going to dress up like Elvis but now I don't even want to go."

"Why?"

"You won't believe this. My mom ran into . . . "

"Come on, Winona, spill the beans."

"Ericka Gussen."

"Who?"

"Ericka Gussen. Remember? I've told you about her."

"Ericka . . . Holy shit, your 'husband'?"

"Yup."

"She hot?"

"I didn't ask but guess what my mother did?"

"Don't tell me, Winona the Nurse invited her to Candy tonight."

"Affirmative."

"Wow."

"Girl, I tell you it has been the craziest day."

"Well, I will go back to my question, what are you going to wear tonight? You have to look astonishing, you will have a bride-to-be and a husband waiting for you."

"Asshole. I told you—Elvis."

"Elvis Taylor."

"Dork."

"Ha ha . . . Now, seriously, Winona. You need to get your shit together. You can't be playing with people's feelings anymore."

"You do it all the fucking time."

"There's one big difference between you and me. I'm single and you aren't."

"But you still hurt people's feelings. You hurt me."

"Are you kidding me? You going to play the

you-hurt-me thing again? You knew, everyone does, things with me never turn into a relationship."

Tori pulls her hair up into a ponytail and looks at herself in the mirror. I lay down on the bed, looking at the ceiling. She, like, reads my mind because she says, "Answers are not on the ceiling. Grow balls, Winona. Be straight with Rebecca."

Tori bends and kisses me softly on my lips. Then, she grabs her stuff and says, "I'll see you tonight. We'll deal with Rebecca, Ericka Gussen, and that Cherry Pie of yours."

Tori walks out of the room leaving the scent of jasmine and doubt in the air. What am I going to do? I can hear the computer's beeping. Cherry Pie asking for my attention on the chat. I log out from my website and turn my computer off. I'll finish recording later. I'm tired. I deserve a nap.

CHAPTER SIX
four p.m.

"Hello?"

"Wonnie, what the fuck? I've been trying to call you all day."

"Sorry, Babe. I was taking a nap—had my phone on silent. It's been a rough day and . . . "

I couldn't even continue, she went, "I don't understand what's up with you. We have an amazing night, then, as soon as I talk about serious issues you just clam up, sneak out of my place, and . . . "

"I didn't sneak out."

"Really? Cause the way I see it you didn't say goodbye or anything."

"I texted you earlier, didn't I? Come on, Rebecca,

cut me some slack here." She doesn't say anything. I continue, "I'm very sorry, really it's been a crazy day. You can't imagine, Baby." I use the softest voice I can find, Rebecca hardly ever gets mad, but when she does it's pretty hard to make her get out of it.

"So, what's wrong with Dylan?"

"Cancer."

"No! For reals? How's your mom?"

"Not well."

"I can imagine. And you, how are *you*?"

"I'm fine. I mean, he's old after all."

"Yes, but he's Dylan."

"I'm trying not to think too much about it, make things easier."

Rebecca stays quiet for a bit, and then she asks, "Is that what you are doing with us?"

"What do you mean?"

"Trying not to think about it."

"I dunno. I guess."

* * *

Before Rebecca and her brother moved out of her parents' home things were really rough. First, Vinny came out, and then she did. Her father started blaming Vinny for it, According to Rebecca's old man, if it hadn't been for his son being gay, his daughter would have never started hanging out in that place, and I quote, "full of fags and dykes." Rebecca had had it; she emptied out her savings, asked for more hours at her job and started looking for an apartment.

Rebecca was told at The Basement she had to become Vinny's legal guardian. I told her I could have Dad help her. He was in town and she really needed advice on how to become Vinny's legal guardian. Dad, moved by the whole situation, even hired a friend of his in Philadelphia to handle her case.

Rebecca didn't have to pay one cent for the whole thing. It wasn't an easy process, but things worked out in the end and Rebecca became Vinny's legal guardian.

The first part of Rebecca and Vinny's new life was legally solved. But then it became hard, living on their own. They had *nothing* but their laptops, two suitcases with clothes and shoes, a box with books, and some very basic household items.

Everyone at The Basement helped them: mattresses, sofas, tables, and kitchen stuff were put in their places. My mom and I helped out too.

I don't know how she does it. Rebecca takes classes at the community college at night, makes sure Vinny does well in school, works all day and finds time to put some hours in at The Basement. She started just as a volunteer, but Sonia saw her potential and taught her everything she knew, then she included her in the application of this giant grant which would guarantee a salary for Rebecca.

My girlfriend's role at The Basement is essential. She's being paid to coordinate workshops for teens. She wants to be a psychologist, and wants to provide therapy for the LGBT community.

She's awesome. Man, sometimes I wonder, what's she doing dating me? She deserves better.

* * *

"So, what did your mom say about our plans?"

"What do you mean?"

"Us. Getting married." I can't believe Rebecca was expecting me to tell my mom about *her* plans. I say nothing.

"Well?" she asks.

"I didn't say anything."

"How come?" Rebecca sounds surprised. "Maybe that would cheer her up."

This is when I lose it. "It wasn't the right time."

"There will never be a right time. Some things you just have to say whenever."

"What the fuck, Rebecca? I haven't even said yes!"

"But I thought we . . . "

"Listen, Rebecca, us getting married is *your* idea, not mine."

"So you're telling me you *don't* want to marry *me?*"

"Look, Rebecca, what I'm trying to say is . . . "

"No, I get it. You don't want to."

"It isn't like that. It's just . . . I'm just . . . confused. I'm confused."

"Confused, seriously? I know what's going on, Wonnie. The second you see this taking a more serious road, you bail out."

"I'm not bailing out." I'm about to lose my patience, so I breathe in before saying anything else. "Listen, Rebs. Let's meet later to talk like we agreed. We shouldn't be talking about this on the phone. Why don't we have dinner, like you suggested? Rebecca? You there?"

* * *

Rebecca would fix the world if she could. You should hear the speech she says every time she starts a workshop:

"Being a teen isn't easy, you have a lot on your

plate: friends, parents, school, body changes, drama-drama-drama. And if that isn't enough, you have one more thing to deal with—being queer. I want you to hear me and record it in your mind: you're not alone."

Kids feel comfortable with her right away, especially the middle schoolers. They follow her like bees to honey. She just gets them. She says she sees Vinny in every one of them. She doesn't want anyone going through the rough times her brother went through. She's one brave girl. Not only did she face her own parents when she and Vinny came out, she faces lots of angry parents every day. She helps them understand that it's okay to feel shocked at first, but having a queer kid is completely fine.

The thing is when it comes to her own shit, Rebecca isn't as mature as one would imagine. The Cheerleader Type comes out and she does crap like yelling, hanging up the phone, slamming doors, and walking off.

When we started dating she would break up with

me every couple of weeks. She wouldn't understand this weird relationship that I have always had with Tori or the fact that I wanted to be with the whole gang instead of hanging out just the two of us. I love Rebecca. I'm lucky to have her in my life. I love how passionate she is about *her* projects and about *my* projects. It's great to spend the weekends at her place and just fool around with her and Vinny but . . . getting married is different.

I have thought about moving in with her. It makes sense, plus, I would stop being Mama's little girl and would start a life of my own. But I have never talked about this with her.

Maybe Tori is right. Maybe I have to let her go. Maybe I do need to get my shit together. I'll let her chill out. Then I'll send her a cute text and she'll be fine. It always works that way. Then, we'll see.

* * *

I sit down at my desk. I still have a podcast to finish. I turn on my computer and the first thing I see is a message from Cherry Pie:

Is the *Come Out!* star coming to Candy tonight? I would like to meet her.

Cherry Pie is totally flirting with me. I should ignore it. I should . . . But I'm weak, and curious.

She's no star but, yes, she going to Candy. I pause, then add, And she might be dressing up like Elvis.

Kinky. Can't wait.

I should log out. I should simply say, K, will see you tonight, bye. But instead I go:

How about you Cherry Pie? What will he be wearing?

This is not the most subtle way to find out if Cherry Pie is one of those gay dudes who likes fooling around with dykes like me.

Well SHE was thinking about Dorothy from The Wizard of Oz, but if you are going to be Hollywooding tonight, maybe Cherry should try Marilyn.

Marilyn sounds hot.

I'm still not sure. What if Cherry is a queenie who refers to himself as she?

It does, doesn't it? Hey, did you read the book I recommended to you?

I did, I'm including it in my next podcast.

Which is what I should be finishing up, instead of chatting here. It is always the same—once I start I can't stop.

Are you going to continue with bisexuality on your podcast?

Yeah. I got a lot of comments last time.

Yeah, bi is always controversial.

It is. Are you bi?

Wow, you are right on target!

Haha. Come on, tell me more about yourself Cherry Pie. What's your real name?

Why don't we save this conversation for later tonight?

Sure thing.

✳ ✳ ✳

Before The Basement, I thought that there were only gay men and lesbian girls. I did not know about transgender. I did not know that we all come in different colors and flavors: alternaqueers, twinks, bears, queens, studs, femmes, bois, etc . . .

The more I learned about people like me, the more I learned to like myself. I learned to simply be myself. I started paying more attention to what I wore and what I looked like. I'm what people call "butch." I cut my hair short on the sides but I keep a long wave on the top. I used to dye it with funky colors but now I just let it be. I wear jeans or Dickies and plain t-shirts most of the time.

I have been confused for a gay guy. I don't mind when it happens. I guess you can say I look more like a metrosexual. I like getting manicures and shaving my armpits and legs, not that I wear skirts or dresses, but if you have ever been in Philadelphia in the summer, you know that the only way to survive is with a good pair of shorts.

Tori, for example, plays around more with her style. She can be butchy one day and a total lipstick the next. She likes spicing it up. That's part of her charm. Rebecca is a femme. She likes wearing vintage dresses, which I call hipster dresses just to make her mad. She's a beautiful brunette with blue eyes and strawberry lips. I like it when she puts her hair up and wears those old lady glasses and superbright red lipstick. Feels like I'm dating a pin-up girl from the fifties.

Seriously, I don't know what she's doing with me.

I check what I have recorded so far. I think I will just add one more song and I'm done.

* * *

"Wonnie, you here?" That's my mom knocking on my door.

"Yeah, come on in." Her hair is a mess. I can see the pillow marks on her face. "What's up?" I ask.

"Thought you were going out."

"No, I'm doing my podcast. Then I'll go to Candy."

"Jesus, I forgot to wash your Elvis thing for tonight."

"*Mom*."

"Don't give me crap—I'm not your maid. How many times do I have to tell you that?"

She's right, I'm fucking lazy. I always expect her to do my shit. "Okay, okay, I'll do it right now. You going out?"

"Yeah, I wanna check on Dylan and then I'm meeting Tala and Dakota."

"Oh, you are going? I'm glad. They will cheer you up."

She's about to leave the room, but stops, and with a smile says, "Hey, can you also wash my scrubs?"

"Sure."

"You know what? Why don't you just do all this laundry since you are here? I have two full baskets of clothes in the basement."

"But . . . "

"Thank you, darling. Love having you here. Now

I gotta take a quick shower to wake up and then I'm off." Mom looks at me. I guess she sees something on my face because she asks, "You okay?" This is my chance, this is it.

"Mom . . . "

"Yes?"

I have to—I have to tell her about this whole shit with Rebecca, but . . .

"Nothing."

"Nothing is always something, Wonnie."

"I know. It's not important. We'll talk later, okay?" I'm such an idiot.

"Sure. Hey, I'm sorry if I was rough on you today at the vet's."

"No worries. Text me and tell me how the old guy is doing."

Wonnie'sWorld

HERE COMES THE BRIDE
(ONLY SHE'S IN A TUXEDO)

I was married once. I was eight years old and she was nine. I was the wife and she was the husband. It was easy because our kids were made of plastic and they never complained about our parental practices. Also, we had no mortgage, and no debts whatsoever. I bet you have been married like this before. Think back to your childhood: that game with this or that girl, this or that boy. You know, when you were playing house. Or maybe you did it alone. Maybe you were a single parent to your Barbies or your Bratz; pushing your baby in your plastic stroller all around your block. How easy it was, right? The easiest marriage in the world. Easier than the one you saw at home with your parents. If you fought with your partner or if your plastic kids misbehaved, you just stopped the game and that was that. No need for a marriage counselor or a lawyer.

Marriage, real marriage is not a game. Real marriage is supposed to be for life. Real marriage is about the serious agreement you make with your loved one to be together in good times and bad. Girls are always dreaming of getting married. Believe it or not I did too. I guess I wanted my Polly Pockets, the most amazing dolls in the world, to have the perfect family. Perfect family, right? As a Polly Pocket mother, I sucked. Ask me where my daughters are and I will say one word: LOST.

When I think of marriage now I don't picture me as the bride with all her Polly Pockets holding my bridal train. Geez, I don't even see myself wearing a dress. If I picture myself getting married, I see me wearing a tuxedo, my old red Converses, and a red bow tie. I see myself smiling for the camera. I see myself checking out the bridesmaids. Where is the bride in this image of my future? Who is she?

No clue.

I'm a little bit lost today. There is a wonderful woman in my life and she wants us to be together. She wants us to be wife and wife. But I'm not even nineteen years old yet, and I can't decide whether I want my coffee with regular or soy milk, you know #FirstWorldProblems. What to do? What to do?

Posted by Wonnie T.
June 21st | 6:02 pm | No Comments

150

CHAPTER SEVEN

six p.m.

I STARTED MY BLOG LIKE FOUR YEARS AGO. IT WAS born like every other blog: as a way to let it all out, my urgent realities, my massive ups and downs. It's a place to vent. It's always been like talking to someone about my life.

I sometimes like reading random posts from the past. My past. Most of the time I feel silly and stupid for what I wrote, but sometimes I discover a different me in my writing—bright, smart, words written by Wonnie Taylor. Tori has told me that I should use all the material from my blog to write a novel. *A Dyke is Born,* she says I should call it. I don't see myself as a writer. I like music and I like media more than literature.

When I wrote in my blog that I was taking a year off, people posted many comments. Some of them invited me to think things over but most of them encouraged me to do so; someone told me it was a mature, smart move.

I believe not many young people know for real what they want to do with their lives. Many just choose whatever career their parents have and many just choose according to the trend of the season. My mom says that when the Indiana Jones movies came out, everyone in her class wanted to become an archeologist. It's not like I don't know what to do; I'm actually already doing what I want to do in life. I'm even making good money out of it. The thing is, I want to get more experience in what I do, and I'm just not ready to leave Philadelphia.

This city, this city is my soul. I'm not ready to give up on her. Yes, Philadelphia is also a constant topic on my blog. Cruising in Philadelphia is like cruising in my life.

I can't procrastinate anymore. So I better get to it.

I hate doing laundry. I can't imagine what the world was like before washing machines. I know it's just about throwing your clothes in, adding the soap, and pushing some buttons, *but* Mom has always done it for me. I don't know how she puts up with me. I disappear for a few days and when I come back it seems like I bring a month's worth of dirty clothes and then, almost magically, my clothes are clean and folded the next day on my bed. Mom complains. She tells me I'm a pig, she wonders how she raised a pig, and she's amazed that girls want to date this pig.

Today this pig needs to wash clothes. So I make myself some iced tea and go to the basement, a.k.a. the storage and laundry room. I haven't been here in ages.

I pull out my Elvis outfit. Aunt Tara made it for me two years ago. I wore it for a Halloween party in high school and then I buried it in my closet.

It stinks. I add some other white clothes from the basket. That is as much as I know, white clothes go together. My mom opens the door upstairs and yells, "I think I left some clothes in the dryer, can you take them out and fold them, darling?"

Darling is the word my mother uses when she asks me for something. Rebecca's word is *Sweetheart*. She uses it the same way my mom does, when she wants me to do something she knows I hate.

I take the clothes out of the dryer and start folding shit. For a few minutes I think of nothing but getting this chore done. Maybe that is why we fold clothes; it is like yoga, you have to be so focused.

In the storage part of the basement is this old chair. It used to be my favorite thinking spot when we lived in Baltimore. I sit down on it and make it my working space. I check Twitter on my smartphone and look for #Candy, today's trending topic. I read people's posts about tonight's event.

* * *

The buzzer of the washing machine wakes me up. I must have fallen asleep. I stand up and as I'm walking to the laundry room I run into a box. "Family Photos," it reads in black marker. My mom's handwriting.

I throw the white clothes in the dryer, then add the second basket of clothes into the washing machine. I'm never going to finish folding all this shit, which is mostly mine. As I continue doing it, I wonder what it would be like to live full time with Rebecca and Vinny. Will we take turns doing our laundry or will we do it all together on Sundays while eating junk food and watching something stupid on TV? Will we have dinner parties with our gay friends from The Basement? Will Rebecca and I introduce each other as, "This is my wife," or will we simply use our first names?

Rebecca. I gotta text her. Even better, I can take a selfie next to my mom's washing machine and send it to her. I type:

Wonnie, The Maid.

Then:

Baby, I'm sorry about how our conversation turned out. I love you very very very much.

Nothing. She's really pissed off. I call Vinny. He'll tell me how the weather is over there.

"Hey, dude. You home?"

"Yeah, watching TV. What's up?"

"Your sister home?"

"She was here, just left. Did you guys fight? She was in a really bad mood. She cleaned the whole kitchen."

When Rebecca is mad, she cleans. She says that when she lived with her parents, she used to throw shit around and break stuff and her mother would clean up. After she and Vinny started living on their own, she realized that throwing a tantrum also meant cleaning up her own mess. "I just did it once and it took me a whole afternoon to pick up the broken glass," she told me.

So now whenever she's really mad, she cleans.

It's not a good sign that she cleaned her kitchen

today. Vinny sounds worried. I tell him, "Yeah man, we did, but everything will be fine. I will dress like Elvis tonight and she will fall for me all over again."

"Fat Elvis in a white suit?" Vinny asks.

"Is there any other?" I say.

Vinny is like the younger brother that I never had. He's been through rough times. Like Rebecca, he spends most of his time at The Basement. He's made friends and we believe he has a crush on this new guy who just started going to the Teen Group.

* * *

I finish folding the clothes. I look at my watch. It's almost seven o'clock. I should take a shower while my outfit is in the dryer. I text Rebecca one more time:

You never told me what would you be wearing tonight. I hope you don't forget I will be Elvis, I'm looking forward to singing in your ear.

No reply.

CHAPTER EIGHT
nine p.m.

I CHECK MY PHONE AS SOON AS I GET OUT OF THE shower. I have only one text from my mom saying Dylan has been sleeping all day. Nothing from Rebecca. I call her and it goes directly to her voicemail. She's still mad. What am I going to do now?

I go downstairs wrapped in the towel to get my costume. As I climb the stairs I see the box with family pictures again. I kneel down, open it, and then close it right away. The box looks at me as if saying, *Take me.* But I don't have time for nostalgia now.

Back in my room, I Google some Elvis Presley images to check out his hairdo. I'm sure I can make something work. The last time I wore it, Rebecca couldn't go, so I asked Tori to be my date. She dressed like Pocahontas, but she looked more like a stripper. She sure was a hit with my friends, showing half of everything. She's sexy and she knows it. She loves the attention.

Tori and I, we are great together. In bed, too. Sex with her is mind-blowing. She lets me do anything I want, at least most of the time. She likes playing the submissive lover, she lays on the bed and lets me take the initiative, which is great, but now that I think about it, it is all about her. All about her pleasure. I disappear. I hear her moaning, asking, but it's like I could be just anyone else. See, with Rebecca, it's wonderful. Not only do we take turns to give and receive, but she also looks me in the eyes, says my name, moans in my ear. I like it when she asks me to do something in particular. "Bite me here," she'll say. Or she won't say a word but will lead my hand, my fingers, my face to wherever she wants me, while begging me with her eyes.

Fuck, now I'm horny. And judging by way things are going, it seems like I won't be getting any.

✳ ✳ ✳

Where the hell did I put my sideburns? There's no point in dressing like Elvis without them. I want to text my mom, but where's my phone? I just had it right here and then . . . Oh, right—I find it in the laundry.

Hey Mom, have you seen my Elvis pork chops?

She doesn't respond, so I text again. You really never pay attention to me, do you?

Still nothing?!

???

Finally, she answers. I told you I would leave them on my dresser, the glue is in the first drawer.

Thanks. You da best!

I go to my mom's room. I get the pork chops from the dresser. I open the drawer, and as I'm looking for the glue, I see a couple of pill bottles

160

and pick one up. *Fluoxetine*, it says. I wonder what that is. I Google the word on my phone and I read the following: "Prozac. Prescription drug. Consult a doctor if you have a medical concern. This medicine is an SSRI that treats depression, obsessive-compulsive disorder (OCD), and other disorders."

Is my mom depressed? Is that what she was trying to talk to me about? I sit down on her bed and I close my eyes and create this long series of scenes of my mom during the last year.

- My mom coming home early from work.
- My mom on the couch with take-out food, watching TV.
- My mom not answering the phone, unless it's one of my aunts.
- My mom in two outfits—her scrubs or her yoga pants.

Fuck. Mom is depressed and I haven't even been there for her. I'm such an asshole. I take my phone and type:

Mom. I love you. You know that?

Wonnie, don't scare me. What did you do?

Nothing, I'm serious. I love you, that's it.

:) Love you too.

Heartbreaks suck, but I guess they suck even more when you are forty-something.

I was nine when Mom and Dad split, everything changed. It was like we had taken off our old lives and put on some new clothes, something that doesn't really fit you until you wear it for a while. The life my mom was wearing looked pretty gray at the beginning. But little by little it started to get color. We moved out of Grandma's and got a small apartment.

Her classmates used to come to our place. My mom's study groups were fun. You could see they were working their asses off but they would laugh all the time too. They would order Chinese food or pizza. My mom was the oldest of the group and everyone—I repeat, *everyone*—would confide in her for any type of problems, you know: grades, parents, boyfriends, girlfriends, lovers, you name it.

I was so proud of her. I know Dad was too. When he called me he would always ask how she was doing. "You be good to your mom, Wonnie," he would say. "School is really important for her and she needs to focus on that."

"I know Dad," I would reply.

But it was Dad who wasn't all that good; my mom kept worrying about him. First, because he was depressed without us; then, because he worked way too much; also, because of his girlfriends.

I have a billion examples of how my mom is the best. It worries me that she has been feeling like shit and I haven't even bothered to notice.

I've finished getting ready. It's almost time to go. I take a selfie and upload it to both Twitter and my Facebook.

Elvis is ready to rock 'n' roll, Girlz!

CHAPTER NINE
nine thirty p.m.

EVEN WITH ALL THE MESS, I'M EXCITED ABOUT TONIGHT'S party. It took weeks and weeks for all of us from The Basement to prepare for it. Everyone from our community is going to be there. It will be the biggest pre-gay parade event of the year.

I'm early. The doors haven't opened yet, but there are already a bunch of people waiting in line. I take some pictures with my phone because one rarely has a chance to see Benjamin Franklin, Fidel Castro, and Lady Gaga (or is it Marilyn Manson?) all in one spot. There's also a Captain America, Anna and Elsa from *Frozen*, three Ninja Turtles, and one, two, three, four . . . well, a bunch of zombies. I see

Sonia. She's a beautiful Sleeping Beauty. She gets me past the line.

"You're Basement family. What're you doing out here?" she says.

The place looks wonderful. I didn't know how Rebecca pulled this off. I guess having Jeff and Daniel help her was smart. Those gays can make anything happen. They don't get called Martha Stewart for nothing.

The place has a beach motif—you know, with white and navy stripes, umbrellas, and chaises. The lights of the dance floor are blue and their flickering makes you feel like you are in the middle of the ocean.

Tori's already here. She looks handsome in her biker outfit—stretch black faux-leather pants, jacket, boots, and the most outrageous makeup ever.

"You a Harley mama or a hooker?" I say.

"Shut the fuck up and give me a kiss," she says. "I'm a Sons of Anarchy chick," she says, smiling.

"How are you Winona—I mean, Elvis? You feeling better?"

"Yeah, well, not really, but what can I do? Hey, have you seen Rebecca?"

"I haven't, but I know she's here. It seems she's been bossing Jeff and Daniel around." Tori cracks an invisible whip.

"Right."

"Did you talk to her?" Tori asks.

"Sorta. It didn't go so well. She hung up on me," I say.

"Fuck."

"Yes, fuck."

"Do you want a sip of this?" Tori pulls a flask out of her jacket.

"What is that?"

"Don't ask, just drink."

"If Sonia sees you, she'll kill you."

"Well, she'll kill many others, believe me. I'm not the only one who found a way to break the no-alcohol rule. Come on, just a sip," Tori insists.

She looks around, opens the flask and makes me take a swig.

"You need it," she says as I drink.

"Is that tequila?" I ask.

"No, it's Mezcal. A friend brought me a bottle from a trip to Mexico City."

"Man, I can't feel my tongue," I say laughing. "I'm telling you, Tori, if Sonia finds out . . ."

"Shhh. Besides, I told ya, I'm not the only one. You just pay attention to Martha and Stewart," Tori says. Then she points to the entrance and says, "Finally, let's get this party started!" The doors are now open and a parade of funny-looking people start coming in.

I have to find Rebecca before the place gets too crowded. I wonder what she's wearing? She kept saying, "I want it to be a surprise."

I leave Tori and go look for Rebecca at the DJ's booth and in the kitchen. Nothing. Where is she?

This building used to be a restaurant, and then it was turned into a dance club, now they rent it out for events and parties. It's a huge, old, two-story building with a very classic Philly row-house look from the outside, but ultra modern on the inside. The second floor is an open terrace where you can see what's happening below; perfect for those who prefer chatting to dancing. Perfect also for making out. It looks empty from here.

What if she's in the bathroom finishing up her makeup? Rebecca likes perfection and she can take hours in front of a mirror. I'm on my way there when this velvety voice calls my name, "Wonnie?"

I find a tall girl with a blonde wig, halter-style white dress, red lips . . . an amazing Marilyn Monroe.

"Yes?" I ask while I admire her slim figure with long, strong legs. She's wearing the sexiest open-toe stilettos. "Do I know you?" I ask her.

"You do and you don't." The girl says, getting close to me and grabbing both my hands. "I'm . . . "

"Don't tell me, you are Cherry Pie," I say.

The girl smiles and nods.

"Nice to meet you, Cherry Pie," I tell her.

"I can't believe I found you so easily," she says, which means she was actually looking for me. How flattering.

"Yeah, well . . . " I don't know what to say. I can feel my cheeks getting hot. I'm a bit embarrassed. "Well, I would love to hang out with you now but there's . . . I'm . . . I need to do something."

"What are you up to?" she says while putting her hand on my shoulder.

"I'm looking for . . . someone." Shit, I should've said, "looking for my girlfriend."

"Maybe I can help you find that *someone*," Cherry Pie says, smiling. She's hot. She has these big beautiful eyes and . . .

"Hey, have we met before?" I ask her.

"Why? Do I look familiar?" she asks while getting closer to me. She rests her hands on my shoulders again and smiles. I guess she notices that I freak out a bit because she lets me go a second later.

"Yeah. I don't know. Maybe. Your eyes . . . " But then the music gets louder and louder, more and more people are around us. She says something but I can't understand.

"Hey, Elvis, I see you found your woman," Tori shouts. She then looks at Cherry Pie and says, "Oh, you're not Rebecca."

"I can't find her," I yell.

"Who's Rebecca?" Cherry Pie asks.

Tori takes a good look at her before saying, "Hi, my name is Tori, what's yours?"

"She's Cherry Pie," I yell.

"Oh, *you* are Cherry Pie." Then Tori looks at me. "And you are in deep shit," Tori says giggling. She then yells, "Oh, that's my song!" "Bad Girls" by M.I.A is playing.

"Cherry, let's dance." Tori grabs Cherry Pie's hand, and doesn't give her a chance to say no. I wave goodbye and continue my search for Rebecca.

More and more people start arriving. I see like five members of the Avengers, two more Ninja Turtles, or are they the ones from earlier? I also see an Abraham Lincoln holding hands with a vampire, two Michael Jacksons, and a couple of dragged-out Disney princesses. No sign of Rebecca.

"Hey, Wonnie, looking good!" Jeff says. His blond curly hair has turned into a dark bob with a white flower on the side. A long pearl necklace and a tight black dress complete his outfit. He's a queenie from the twenties.

"Man, how did you fix your hair like that?" Daniel says while touching my hairdo. He's some sort of peacock, in blue spandex with some long feathers coming out of his back. Across his chest he has a small purse.

"Well, you know . . . " I say.

"No, I don't. Your hair is *always* a mess." Daniel says. Jeff interrupts him, "Shut up, Dan, she isn't *always* a mess." And he laughs. They're cool, but sometimes they are just bitches.

"Gee, thanks man," I say. "Hey, have you seen Rebecca?"

Jeff and Daniel exchange looks. Both of them cross arms and face me.

"Whaaat?" I ask.

"You are *blah, blah, blah* heart," Daniel says. The music goes louder again and I can't understand him.

"What?" I ask him.

"I said, *you are breaking our girl's heart*," Daniel repeats.

"You better *blah, blah, blah*, Wonnie. *Rebecca loves you very much.*" Jeff adds. A weird remix of "Beware of the Boys" starts to play and can't think of a better song for this moment.

"I love Rebecca, you know that," I say. "Just tell me where she is."

Daniel points at the bar and Jeff points at the balcony on the second floor. Then, both of them mimic some sort of *I-don't-know* with their shoulders. Bar or balcony? I look up, some people are there, sitting on the tables, checking out those who are already dancing. Jeff and Daniel wave goodbye and go to the dance floor.

"Wait, what is she wear . . . ?" Too late, they left.

I'm on my way upstairs when someone pulls my arm. *Now what?* I think. It's Tori.

"Winona, there's something you need to know," she says right in my ear.

"Hey," says Cherry Pie, grabbing Tori's arm. "Your friend here dragged me to the dance floor and then left me." Tori seems a bit off.

"What's going on, Tori, you okay?" I ask her.

"Yeah, yeah, it's just . . . " Tori looks at me and then at Cherry Pie.

"It seems I surprised her by telling her my real name," Cherry Pie adds, smiling, but before she can say anything else, another Marilyn Monroe approaches us. It's Rebecca.

She has a blonde wig and a halter dress, just like Cherry Pie. They look at each other, and then Rebecca looks right at me, and says, "Jeff told me you were looking for me, but I see you found another Marilyn."

"No, wait. Come on, Rebecca . . . "

She looks at Cherry Pie and asks, "Who's this?"

Tori, Cherry Pie and I answered at the same time. Only we say different things.

"Cherry Pie," I say.

"Ericka," Cherry says.

"Ericka Gussen," Tori says. "That's what I was trying to tell you."

"Who are you?" I ask Cherry Pie. I can't believe what I just heard.

"Ericka Gussen," she repeats with a smile.

It takes a few seconds for Rebecca to react, and then she says bitterly, "Wow, so that is why you don't need a wife. You found your lost husband." She starts walking away.

"No, Rebecca, wait." I try to go after her but Tori stops me.

"Let her go. She won't listen to you now." She looks at Cherry/Ericka and adds, "Just solve this," and then goes after Rebecca.

"Wow, it seems that everyone here knows about us."

"Us? There is no *us*," I say.

"You know what I mean," Ericka replies.

Cherry. Ericka. How, why? I don't even know what to ask her. I can't stop looking at her.

"Your mom invited me. Didn't she tell you?"

"I can't be here. I gotta go."

"Relax," she says. "I'm sure your friend Tori can take care of what's-her-name?"

"Rebecca. Her name is Rebecca."

I'm so confused. Is she really Ericka Gussen? I take a good look at her. The costume is in the way, and I cannot see my old childhood friend under those clothes and makeup. She probably reads my mind because she says, "You still can't believe it, right?"

"Well, it's been so long."

Ericka pulls off her wig to show me her black hair hiding under a net. She then looks right at me saying, "Do you recognize me now?"

I finally find the little girl in that woman's face. Yes, it's Ericka Gussen.

"So, that other Marilyn, she's your girlfriend?"

"Yes."

She's about to say something else, instead she looks at the crowd and grabs my hand. "Come on, let's go upstairs. I bet it's less noisy."

Ericka says she started to listen to my podcast because a friend of hers recommended it. She didn't know right away it was me.

"I was figuring myself out, you know? I still am, I guess," she says.

"What do you mean?" I ask her, but she doesn't pay attention to my question, and keeps talking.

"I remember perfectly that first podcast. You were talking about transgender. You were playing songs by—what's his name?"

"Bowie. David Bowie," I say. I have a bad memory for everything in my life except for the music of my podcasts.

"Right. You played a song that I loved; it took me ages to find it. *Hallo Spaceboy.* There's this line that says, 'Don't you wanna be free? Do you like girls or boys? It's confusing these days.' I love it."

"So, when did you find out that it was me making the podcast?"

"It took me a while. And believe me, I checked your website. I even read your blog. I just didn't connect the dots."

"How come you didn't use your real name for my web chat?"

"I dunno. I just used the same username I have always used for everything else in my life."

Ericka keeps looking at me. I guess she, too, is trying to find the little girl in my face. She adds, "I like your podcast and reading your stuff and—"

I interrupt her, "Wait, I gotta stop you there . . . I don't understand why you never told me that *you* were *you*. It doesn't make sense."

"I guess I was waiting for the right moment. Things didn't end all that well between us."

"We were just kids."

"Yes, but we were far from doing kid stuff. You haven't forgotten our games, have you?"

Of course I hadn't forgotten. Ericka was my discovery of sex.

"Did you hear me?" Ericka asks.

I nod. What can I say? I'm anxious; this whole situation is bizarre. Then it strikes me: just earlier today, she was flirting. Wasn't she?

"Today, today it seemed you . . . you were flirting with me," I state.

Ericka lets out a loud laugh and answers, "Ha ha, you think? Maybe, who knows? I don't even know when I do it. My friends say I'm a flirt. They say I even flirt when I order food at the drive-thru."

She's right. She's a flirt. She's doing it right now. Problem is, I'm letting her. I check my phone to see if Tori or Rebecca have called or texted. Nothing.

I take a long look at Ericka and realize I can't be here. I gotta go. I touch Ericka's shoulder and excuse myself. "Hey, I'd love to keep talking to you and catch up, but my life is chaos right now and . . . "

My words seem to throw her off a little, but she

plays it cool. "Sure, I understand. Anything I can do?" Ericka asks, smiling. Damn, she's so pretty.

"No, I just, I have to . . ." I point to the stairs.

"Yes, go, go. Hope everything goes well." Then as I turn to go downstairs she adds, "I will be around, you know . . . in case you . . . you know?"

I wave goodbye and start walking off, and then she yells, "Wonnie, don't forget, I still owe you . . ."

"What? I can't hear you," I say and leave.

The first floor is crazy now. People dancing, people yelling to each other, couples making out. Two boys lean on a wall French kissing while grabbing each other's butts. Three girls exchanging kisses to leave lipstick prints on each other's cheeks. A girl using a boy as a pole to dance on.

This party is certainly heating up.

I can't see Rebecca or Tori anywhere. The lack of illumination does not help. Where the hell were they? I try calling Tori a few times but nothing. I'm desperate. I walk all the way to the bar. To get there, I have to cross the dance floor, which is packed. Before I can get half way, Jeff and Daniel sandwich me.

"Come on, girl, dance, DANCE!"

We are right next to the speakers so I have to yell, "No, no, I can't. I'm looking for Rebecca."

"Whaaa?" yells Jeff.

"Rebecca! I'm looking for her!" I yell into his left ear, and then he tells Daniel something in his ear.

"Oh, still haven't seen her?" Daniel says. "Here, have some of this." Daniel produces a flask and gives me a swig of something that I can't even recognize. Tori was right, it seems like everyone decided to make this party BYOB.

"Stop!" I say.

"You are such a pussy!" Jeff tells me.

Then Daniel adds, "I saw Tori and Rebecca holding hands and heading that way." He points to the ladies' restroom.

"Are you sure?" I ask and Daniel adds, "Yes, they went that way."

"One more sip?" Jeff asks. "You might need it."

"No, no. Thank you."

But they can't take no for an answer and they force me to take another sip. I don't even know what it is, but it feels like a sharp knife cutting my tongue.

Drinking and drugs have always freaked me out a bit. I've heard too many stories both from my mom and the people at The Basement. My grandpa, Mom's father, he died of cirrhosis. Stories say that when he drank he became a horrible man. We never talk about this in the family.

After their divorce, both my parents were bro-kenhearted. Mom just focused on going back to school. But Dad, he was really a mess. That first summer I spent with him, I saw him drinking a lot. I didn't think all that much about it then. It was later, when I learned about Grandpa, that I realized that alcohol was Dad's best friend.

Not once did I see him losing control or anything and I guess that once his life was back in shape he kinda stopped doing it so much.

Anyway, I'm a mess in so many ways and I don't

really care, but drinking has never been my thing. I can take one, two beers, or one, maybe two margaritas, and that's it. If I drink more, I go drunky-pants.

What did those guys give me anyway?

I'm about to go upstairs again, but then decide to try the other restroom. Rebecca isn't there. There's three girls in front of the mirror exchanging lipsticks and blush—the finishing details for their Catwoman costumes. Yes, the three of them are wearing the exact same costume. Another girl is wiping her eyes; she's definitely been crying. She's wearing a long black strapless dress, and she looks like a sad femme fatale.

There are two stalls, but the toilet on one of them is broken, so there are girls waiting for their turn. One of them is dressed like Maleficent; the other one is a G.I. Jane or an Indiana Jones, who knows? I gotta pee, so I stand next to them and wait for my turn.

One of the Catwomen leaves when a girl comes out of the stall. She's dressed like a sexy cop.

Maleficent goes inside the bathroom. G.I. Jane/ Indiana Jones and I wait for our turn. Then crying femme fatale asks us, "Do I look okay now?"

G.I. Jane and I reply, "Yes." But we were both lying, because she is still a mess.

"Thank you," she says and walks out. Then, the door opens again and I see a Marilyn Monroe walking in, question is, is she Rebecca or Ericka? A second later, Marilyn says, "Hey, you." It's Ericka. This Marilyn is Ericka. "Found your girl?"

"No."

Maleficent opens the door and G.I.Jane/Indiana walks in. Maleficent washes her hands and checks her makeup. We can all hear the echo from the music outside and the bass vibrations on the walls. Maleficent walks out.

Ericka stands right next to me. She breaks this uncomfortable silence.

"Are you mad at me?"

"No. Why would I be?"

"I don't know. Maybe because I wasn't honest?"

"Well, that would be a good reason to be mad, right?"

"Yes, of course." She pauses a long time before continuing, "Listen, Wonnie, I'm sorry. I should have . . . "

"Forget it. Shit happens," I say.

"Yeah, it does."

After another long silence Ericka says, "You've always been on my mind, you know."

"How so?"

Ericka leans on the wall. She turns to face me before saying, "You were so important for me. You were my best friend. You were my only friend back then . . . "

"We *all* were friends," I say.

"Come on, Wonnie, you know you and I . . . What we had was special. It was different." All of a sudden, she reaches for my arms and slides her hands down to grab mine. "I didn't know what I was doing then, but I liked you like crazy. I know I was just a child, but . . . it was special, you know?"

I did know.

"I know it might sound stupid or unbelievable," she adds, "I've had many boyfriends, but no one— no one has ever made me feel like I felt with you when we fooled around."

This is turning into something too serious to handle.

"Well, we weren't fooling around. We were married," I say.

Ericka doesn't laugh; she doesn't even smile. She goes, "I've always had this fixation with girls. One friend of mine, he's gay, and he told me I was just bi-curious."

"And are you?" I ask.

"I don't know. I don't think so. I don't know. Maybe you can help me figure it out. I trust you," she says and takes a step closer to me. I know what she's up to.

Suddenly, the door of the stall opened and G.I. Jane/Indiana looks at us, and hurriedly washes her hands before leaving. We are now alone in the bathroom.

As I move towards the toilet, Ericka pushes me to the wall.

"What are you doing?" I say.

"You know what I'm doing," she says before kissing me. Small kisses all over my face, then my lips. I try to stop her, but I can't, I just can't, and I kiss her back. I grab her waist with one hand and the back of her neck with the other. She pulls her arms around me. We become one body. As I caress her back, flashbacks of our childhood start rolling through my head. It all feels so damn good.

"Come here." Ericka takes my hand and leads me into a stall. She puts down the toilet lid and sits me down on it. I'm dumbfounded by what is happening. She sits on my lap; one leg on each side. She lifts her dress and forces my hands to her ass.

"Touch me," she says and starts kissing my neck.

She's wearing a thong, I caress her soft-silky ass. All I can hear is Ericka saying, "Yes, yes!"

Ericka starts to unbutton my shirt. I stop her with both my hands. What am I doing? I wanna leave and, at the same time, I wanna stick my face in her cleavage. She pushes my face into her boobs and all I do is lick them, kiss them. She moans, "Wonnie, oh my god, what are you doing?" I know it's more a surprise statement than an actual question, but it sort of throws me off. I can hear a voice in my head asking exactly the same thing.

I stop. I lift my hands and lean away. Ericka tries to pull me back to her neck but I resist. I say, "No, I can't. I can't." I push Ericka away and stand up.

"But you have to. I need you to. I have to know . . . " She trails off.

"You are fucking crazy, Ericka. Listen, I can't do this," I repeat, "I can't." I open the door and walk out of the stall. Right at that moment Tori pulls Rebecca into the bathroom.

"I was looking for you," I say, and of course at this very moment Ericka walks out of the stall behind me.

Rebecca looks at me, then she looks at her, and says, "Wonnie, how could you?" She then turns at Tori and says, "I'm out of here."

Ericka tries to stop her, saying, "Wait, no, it's not what you think. It was me, it was all me . . . It's my fault, I . . . "

But it's no use. Rebecca storms out of the bathroom. Tori stands there for a second, clueless. She finally says, "What the fuck you doing, Winona?"

"I don't know. I don't fucking know," I say and fall in her arms crying my eyes out.

"I think you should leave," Tori tells Ericka. Ericka walks out. It's only Tori and me in the bathroom.

"What am I gonna do, Tori?" I ask.

"I don't know, sweetie, I don't know."

"Do you have more of that thing?"

"Mezcal?"

"Yes."

"Not much. Rebecca drank more than half of it."

CHAPTER TEN
twelve a.m.

I FEEL LIKE A WOUNDED ANIMAL. AS SOON AS I GET home, I drag myself into my mother's room. The TV is on, but her lights are off. I carefully open the door, wondering if she's up.

"Hey you," she greets me.

"Hey, Mom." I walk in, take off my shoes, and crawl into bed with her.

"What time is it?"

"Midnight."

"And you're back? What is it? Everything okay?" She turns on the lamp on her night table.

"I feel like shit, Mom." I lie my head on her shoulder and start crying.

* * *

Limits. Mom and I end up talking about limits. I haven't set limits in my life, she says, after I tell her what happened tonight.

"I can't believe my daughter is such a love machine," she says trying to make me laugh.

"Shut up, it's not like that," I say.

"It sure sounds like that," she insists. She grabs a tissue from the bedside table, then wipes my eyes and kisses my cheek. "So, what are we going to do?"

"I don't know. I'm sure Rebecca doesn't want to talk to me. She'll never forgive me for what I did."

"You said you didn't do anything with Ericka."

"I didn't. But I did."

"Well, did you or didn't you? Make up your mind, Wonnie."

"I didn't have sex with Ericka, if that's what you're asking, but . . . I did make out with her. It was wrong. I hurt Rebecca's feelings."

"I'm sure you did. Poor Rebecca. Poor girls, both of them. I'm sure Ericka's feelings are hurt, too."

"I don't care about Ericka, Mom."

"Well, you should, she—"

"She went there because of you. You told her about the party, remember?"

"Oh, no, don't you blame this on me. You better focus on how you are going to fix this now."

"Actually, *now* is when *you* tell me what to do," I tell her. My mom pats her lap and invites me to rest my head on it. I do, and she caresses my hair.

"It's weird to have Elvis Presley on my bed," she jokes.

"Mom, come on. This is serious."

"I know, baby, I know. Listen, I can't tell you what to do. You're not a kid anymore. Soon you will be turning nineteen, and when you least expect it you will be independent, living on your own."

"But I always want to be here, at home," I say. I sound like a child. No, I sound like a spoiled child.

"Wonnie, this will always be your home, but you

need to experience the world, to make mistakes and learn from them. You need to grow up."

"Are you telling me I'm immature?"

"I'm telling you that you need to grow up. Face your problems, face Rebecca. If you don't want to marry her, just tell her so."

"But I'll lose her."

"You won't know until you talk to her. Maybe her idea of getting married was just an idea. Who knows? People do weird things when they're afraid."

"Afraid of what?" I ask.

My mom's face changes. It's like she's coming to a realization herself. "Afraid of not being loved the way they love." My mom pauses, then says, "You never asked me what happened with George. Why?"

The question takes me by surprise. I sit up straight and say, "I dunno, I mean, I did try, remember? But you told me to forget George ever happened. So I figured it was something private."

"As private as you telling me you were making out with a girl in a bathroom?" Mom asks me.

"Oh, come on, it's not the same."

"But it is."

"I guess. So, anyway. Why did you guys break up?"

"Because I wanted to get married. I wanted us to be a family."

"And he didn't? What an asshole. Don't feel bad, Mom. It's his loss, anyway."

"Mine too. He didn't want to break up; he just didn't want to get married. He didn't want to live together."

"What?"

"He wanted us to spend more time getting to know each other before taking another step."

"And?"

"And I broke up with him because . . . " Mom sighs and then says, "Because I was afraid he didn't love me the way I loved him. I decided to think he just didn't love me all that much."

"To me it seemed like he did."

"I know. I just . . . I guess I was being a child. Like you. I wanted things to be *my* way."

Tears are leaking from her eyes. It's my turn to reach for the Kleenex and help wipe them away. I look at her. She's so beautiful, but she's had the saddest eyes since she and George broke up. She hasn't been herself. It takes me a few minutes to decide whether I should ask about the pills or not.

"What is it, Wonnie? I can almost see your thoughts baking in that head of yours."

"Are you depressed? Is that why you're taking meds?"

"What? How did you . . . ?" Mom asks me. I point to her drawer. Mom sighs again before saying, "I guess. At first I thought I was only sad, but then I couldn't shake it off, so I decided to accept that I needed help. I started therapy."

"Do you think *I* need therapy? Do you think I'm depressed?" I ask her. My mom smiles at first, but then she gives me a serious look.

She holds my hand and says, "Wonnie, what you need is to grow up."

"Come on, Mom. I'm serious."

"I'm serious too. You need to stop acting like a child, you need to learn to be responsible for your own life. You need to start learning from the consequences of your actions."

She's right. I stay quiet for a minute, then say, "Maybe I should just go with Dad and stay with him for the whole summer, stay there forever."

"Or maybe, before going away like that, you should spend a few days on your own. That will help you decide the next step. No one can help you better than yourself—not Dad or me or Tori or Rebecca." My mom kisses me on the head. "Now go to bed. You're tired. I'm tired. We'll talk tomorrow."

I stand up and walk out. As I open the door, I stop for a second. "Hey, how's Dylan?"

"I thought you weren't going to ask," Mom says. "Dylan . . . he was put to sleep. He was in too much pain."

"Fuck. I'm sorry. Mom are you okay?"

"I'm sad, but it's okay. It was his time."

Tears start down my face again, only this time they're for Dylan, our companion.

"I didn't even get to say goodbye," I tell her.

"I know."

"'Night, Mom."

"'Night, sweetie."

As I walk out of my mom's bedroom I notice a bottle of wine in her trashcan. I look around and notice a glass sitting on her night table. I realize I've seen Mom drinking quite often lately. I've seen this image before, only it wasn't her, it was Dad.

"Hey, should you be drinking wine? You know, considering you're taking meds?" I dare to ask.

Mom looks straight at me, drinks a sip of her wine and says, "Wonnie, you have nothing to worry about, okay?" I nod, and then close the door behind me.

Wonnie'sWorld

SILENT NIGHT, SPOILED NIGHT

On crazy nights when I feel completely lost there's only one safe place, my mother's bed. My mother's bed has rescued me so many times. It's a soft safety net that has prevented me from crashing into little pieces.

My mom's bed and my mom's arms and my mom's words pulled me out of the mud I was sinking into. Mud. Yes.

I got a visit from the past that has put my present and my future at risk. But I don't blame it, no. Sometimes only when you look the past right in the eye you learn how to really say goodbye to it so you can embrace your present and start drafting a future.

My past made me realize that my present is beautiful but messy. Very messy. My present shook, my present cried, my present told me to fuck off. My future is nowhere to be found.

Silent night, spoiled night.

Nothing makes sense anymore.

Posted by Wonnie T.

June 22nd | 2:03 am | No Comments

After I finish writing my post, I turn my computer off, stand up, and go to the bathroom to wash my face. I look at myself in the mirror. Who am I? What have I done?

I turn off the lights in the bathroom and walk to my bed. I look for my pajamas. Shit, they are in the laundry room.

For a second I consider just looking for a shirt and getting into bed. But I have a thing for my PJs. They're soft and fresh, and right now I need soft and fresh.

I go all the way to the basement. I turn on the light, get my pajamas from the basket, and, as I walk out, I see the box of pictures I found earlier that day. I take it with me. Looking at our family pictures might distract me from this stupid night.

Once on my bed, I place the box on my lap and start pulling out photo after photo. Me and my parents in the old Hard Rock Café in Baltimore. Me and my parents at the Oriole Park watching a baseball game. Me and my parents at Hershey

Park. There are some other pictures of us around Baltimore. There are also some pictures of Christmas in Philadelphia. Grandma, my aunts. There are even some pictures of Dylan running around.

I pull out some more photos and I find pictures of me and my mom at Washington Square Park and at the rowing club. Pictures of me and my dad at the National Aquarium in Baltimore. Dylan, my mom, and me walking around the city. Me and my parents at my middle school graduation.

Our pictures could easily be from the catalog of a department store. We are a model family, even though we're not in the same city anymore. Dad and Mom managed to raise me together.

All of a sudden it strikes me. This is what Rebecca wants—a family. This is why she wants to get married. She wants to build with me the family she lost when she moved out. I'm so fucking stupid.

I leave the box on my bed and go to my computer. I start typing.

CHAPTER ELEVEN
three a.m.

MY TELEPHONE WAKES ME UP. IT'S STILL DARK OUTSIDE. I answer. It's Rebecca.

"Hey."

"Hey, you sleeping?"

"Sort of. You okay?"

"Kinda. Can we talk?"

"Please."

"Well, I'm here—outside your house. Come out."

"Hold on."

I put on my slippers and run downstairs. From the door's window I see Rebecca in her Marilyn Monroe dress but without the wig. I open the door.

"Hey, come in."

"No, let's talk out here. It's a nice night." Rebecca sits down on the steps and I sit next to her.

"You sure you don't wanna come in?"

"Yes."

"Are you mad at me?"

"What do you think?

"Listen, Rebecca, I . . . "

"Don't say anything. I'm doing the talking now."

"Okay."

"So, tonight after seeing you with that girl and after thinking about our relationship, I came to the conclusion that you are an asshole."

"I am. I know, and I'm sorry, Reb . . . "

"Shut up, I haven't finished. Wonnie, there are times in life when one has to forgive and forget, but I'm not willing to do so. Not just yet." I have nothing to tell her. She continues, "You are so stupid sometimes, you know? Because I love you, Wonnie. I love you very much, and it's too painful to see that you're not on the same wavelength. Don't say that you love me—I know you do, but your idea of love is different than mine. I know you sometimes feel attracted to other people. To me, it means it's not working between us. It's like I'm not enough."

"Oh no, baby, no. It's just . . . "

"You wanna be like Tori. You wanna be a bad girl. That's why you fool around with other women."

"Rebecca, I . . . "

"Don't try to deny it. I know. I know and . . . I haven't been all that honest with you."

"What do you mean?"

"I had sex with someone else too."

"Rebecca, you don't have to tell me all this. I . . . "

"I know I don't have to, but I want you to know. It was just weird. This whole thing is all so new for me, for the both of us."

"New?"

"Yes. Just because you had a girlfriend when you were thirteen, and you've slept around like a whore . . . "

"A whore? You're calling me a whore?"

"Yes, I am and shut up—I'm not done. What I'm trying to say is you're not as experienced as you think. Especially when it comes to actual relationships. This is new for *both* of us and I guess I sort of understand you wanted to rock and roll."

"Rock and roll?" I laugh.

"You know what I mean," Rebecca says. "Anyway, sleeping with someone else didn't feel right to me. I felt guilty. I was not betraying you; I was betraying myself and what I believe. And I couldn't stand it."

"Rebecca, I . . . "

"I wanna have sex with someone who loves me, with someone I love. I want commitment and I guess that is why I proposed to you. I wanted to feel you were in this as much as I was."

"But I was. I mean, I am."

"Yes, but on your own terms. Not on mine."

"I don't know if I'm understanding you, Rebs."

"The point is, Wonnie, I was wrong. I realize now I don't really wanna get married."

"Wow, Rebs, that's great. I don't want to get married either, we should . . . "

"I haven't finished, damn it! I don't want to get married, but I also don't wanna be with you. I love you, but I just can't do this anymore."

"Rebecca, are you . . . breaking up with me?"

"Yes, I'm breaking up with you, but not because of what happened tonight. I'm breaking up with you because I deserve better."

"Fuck you."

"No, Wonnie, fuck you. I don't deserve this, all this cheating and . . . "

"Rebecca, I . . . you know I love you, you're just overreacting."

"Am I?"

I just look at her, speechless.

She continues, "I need to put an end to this. I already have so much shit going on. I don't need this. I don't, Wonnie."

Once Rebecca has let it all out, she sighs. She starts to cry. I tell her, "I'm sorry, Rebs, I really am. I wish I hadn't dragged you into my own shit. I . . . "

"You didn't. I walked in myself," she says, and she places her left hand on my lap. I put my right hand on top of hers. I expect her to move it away, but she doesn't.

Then I dare to say, "Can we—can we still be friends?"

"No, Wonnie, we can't," she moves her hand away. She cleans her eyes and then adds, "We can be friendly, just not friends. You understand, don't you?"

"I do."

"Wonnie, you need to get your shit together. You need to grow up."

"Everybody seems to think that."

Rebecca stands up, and then says, "Listen, I'd better go."

Rebecca kisses my cheek. She caresses my hair and I can smell her scent, not her perfume but her own scent.

"Oh, Rebecca, don't do this, not now. It's late, let's talk about this tomorrow. Stay here tonight."

"No, Wonnie. I gotta go." Rebecca starts walking down the steps.

I stand up and ask her, "Hey, who did you have sex with?" Rebecca turns around and looks at me. I can see a big *Really?* in her eyes. She says nothing and continues walking.

Rebecca is right. She deserves better, way better.

I stay outside my house watching Rebecca walk away. I see how she becomes a small white dot far down the street. I wait until she disappears from sight before going back inside.

On my way to my room, I decide to sneak into Mom's room. Yes, I wanna go and sleep with her. I used to do it all the time when we first moved into this house.

The TV is on. She's sound asleep, but she has no

blankets. As I pull covers over her, I notice a strange color on the side of her face. The stain flows onto her pillow and continues down the left side of the bed. Is this vomit?

"Mom?"

Nothing.

"Mom, are you okay?"

I shake her, but she doesn't react. I turn on the light. There's a mess surrounding her body. What's happening?

"Mom? Mom, you're scaring me. Mom, wake up. Mom!"

Did she pass out? I have to call 911.

CHAPTER TWELVE
nine a.m.

I'M GLAD I DECIDED TO CALL MY AUNTS. AT LEAST I'M not alone in the hospital. We haven't seen Mom. A nurse just came and told us they had to pump her stomach. She's still under observation.

My aunts are as nervous as I am. I have explained everything to them and they still don't seem to get it. "But she was just fine," they keep saying.

It's true, Mom seemed fine earlier. I can't believe it. Just a few hours ago we were solving the world's problems in her room.

Yes, we were both sad about Dylan, but nothing seemed unusual. Yes, I found her pills, yes, I saw her drinking, but she told me not to worry. She seemed to have everything under control.

This must be an accident, I know Mom would not try to . . . you know, she would have never dared to hurt herself. Aunt Tala goes to get us coffee. Aunt Dakota is right by my side, holding my hand.

"I feel like shit," I tell her. "I've been so involved in my own shit that I completely ignored Mom."

"Don't blame yourself. I'm sure there must be a logical explanation for all this. We all knew your mother was having a hard time since she and George broke up, but not once did she seem to be out of control."

Aunt Tala arrives with the coffee, and says, "You know, I was thinking, the signs were all there, right in front of us. She seemed *off* more and more frequently. She barely went out. I don't know. I think we all just looked the other way."

"That's exactly what Wonnie says, but blaming this on us won't solve anything," Aunt Dakota says.

We are all quiet now. We all just stay there, drinking our coffee and hating the guts of this fucking waiting room.

* * *

We just got home. My aunts drove us here. They are making soup and tea for my mom while I clean Mom's room. Mom's resting in the living room. She hasn't said a word, and none of us has dared to ask her anything. As I run downstairs to wash her sheets and clothes, I stop to see how she feels. She's sitting down, watching the TV, only the TV is off. I ask her, "Can I bring you anything?"

"No, Tala brought me water. What're you doing? What's that?"

"Your sheets. I'm washing them."

"You are?"

"Yes, you will sleep tonight with clean, fresh sheets."

Mom smiles, then pats the sofa and asks me to sit

next to her. It's like she is ready to talk now. I leave the sheets on the floor and go to her. Before she says a word I say, "You don't have to say anything."

"What do you mean?"

"You don't need to explain what happened. It was all an accident, I know."

"Well, yes, you're right. It was just an accident. I was very stupid, but I do need to talk about it with you."

"Mom, you don't . . . "

"Wonnie, I know you don't want to hear all about it. I know this is a lot for you, but . . . "

"No, it's not. It's okay, shit happens." I try to stand up, but my mom pulls me back to the sofa.

"Oh, Wonnie. Maybe you're right. Maybe shit happens and, yes, it was an accident, but I've been reckless. I'm a nurse, I knew I wasn't supposed to mix meds and alcohol, but I just kept doing it."

"What do you mean you kept doing it? This has happened before?"

"It happens almost every night, I can't sleep, so I take wine and my meds."

"Mom, you . . . what?"

"I need help. I need to take control of my life again. I can't afford to be so reckless." Mom's eyes start watering. She wipes them and continues, "I'm thinking of taking a break from work. I can afford not to work for a month. I might even go to rehab."

"Rehab? Mom you don't need that. Just stay here, I'll help you . . . "

"You?"

"Yes. Give me a chance to help you out. We can deal with this together, and I can go to your group with you. Whatever you need, Mom."

Mom smiles, and hugs me. Then she says, "We'll see what's best."

I kiss Mom on the forehead, and then head for the laundry room. As I put everything in the washing machine, I break down and cry. So this is what it means to be an adult.

It's the end of the world as I knew it. I go to my

chair. I sit cross-legged on it and allow myself to cry as much as I want. I don't cry for what happened with Rebecca. I don't cry for what happened to my mother. I cry because I can't be a child anymore. This was my last day as one.